For Love of Mister Cotton Tail

A Sun and Moon Adventure Series

Table of Contents

"Candy coated chocolate bunnies. Egg. Ending. Hole. Bunny Hill. Queen. Not mad. Mirror. Fall. All fall. Fire. Winter. Egg. Chocolate. Candy. Wonder. Rabbit. Hatter. Red. Hearts." Cotton handed the book back. "Who wrote it?"

This is part of a 10 book long novella romantasy series. *It means the running time is usually an hour to two hours to read for each fantasy romance book. (20k-40k. Sometimes they technically turn into novels at 44k.)*

This is a closed door romance that can be read in two ways: As a standalone, or as a series.

If you read the chapters with just this symbol, you can read this book as a standalone. Enjoy the full romance story inside even if you just grabbed it and didn't realize it was a series. If you wish to know more besides that one HEA? Read all of your book and start either collecting books or head to patreon (https://www.patreon.com/cw/ authorserenawalken) where you can read every book there for a low monthly fee.

This book uses fade to black, however, it is graphic in other ways (depression, murder, sacrifice, etc.) and is not meant for super young children. Use your judgment, Humans.

By the way? I will break in again to your reveries from time to time in our many adventures if you do seek to stick around from book to book.

Or perhaps I won't?

Toodles for now,

Jack Frost

SUN TURNS INTO A NIGHTMARE

"Candy, you must prevent the apocalypse."

Candy turned. She'd never heard the word apocalypse before, but she was five. She had a lot of new words she didn't know. "What is apocalypse?"

"Oh. You are young."

Candy groaned and stood up. It was Michael. "No, leave me alone." She started to run away. Michael had the biggest case of cooties! One time when they were at the playground, he stuck his finger in his mouth and pushed it in her ear.

"Wait, Candy." Michael took off for her. "I am not who I appear to be. When you get older, you must prevent the apocalypse."

"Get away, Michael, I'll tell on you!" Candy touched her nose and stuck out her tongue.

"Candy, don't do this. I don't want to scare someone so young," Michael said. Like he meant that? She knew he loved to scare and annoy the kids at the playground. "Okay then, I'm sorry."

Candy stopped running as the dirt in front of her fell in. From that moment on, things just went from bad to worse.

OUT OF CANDY'S NIGHTMARE

Dominic glared at Nightmare King. "That was so uncalled for!" he yelled. He knew that Nightmare King would interrupt the dream if Candy didn't listen. He had done it before, and he considered it help. Sometimes it was, but sometimes it wasn't.

He had came at an odd time for Candy, she had only been five years old. He was twenty years early, for some reason, and a form that she hated. When she ran, Nightmare King interfered with his nightmares. The poor child screamed as dead fairies fell on her, zombies reached out for her and dragons chased her. He wouldn't have been surprised if it made her wet herself. At that age, he would have to see all that. "Nightmare King! What's the big idea?" Dominic took the initiative to flip him off, something he had never done, but Nightmare King definitely deserved.

"What?" Nightmare King asked innocently.

"Twenty years too early. A form she hated. Sending her all those nightmares!" Dominic was steamed, that was wrong. "She won't sleep for a week, and she's too young to remember or make sense of what I could even say!"

"She'll figure it out when she gets older then. Unless you want to go back in?"

"Not at five years old. Why did you take me to her at five years old?"

"When are you going to tell me what you've been hiding in your pocket?"

Dominic felt his back pocket, remembering the scroll Apocalypse Moon gave him. Everything she knew. He had learned many different things that would help him on the journey. He wasn't clueless, at the mercy of the dimension holes anymore. He even knew why he was called Apocalypse Sun.

Now, he sort of wished he didn't. At some point in his life, one of the destined lovers would call him Apocalypse Man. At that time, fate would intervene, and he and Apocalypse Moon were bound to be enemies. He had no friends except Apocalypse Moon, so the thought was unsettling. There was little she could do that would make him ever feel such a way.

"Are you going to keep pretending with me? Or do you enjoy seeing Candy as her kindergarten bully?"

What an ass. "You're an ass."

"You are getting awfully brave with me, Apocalypse Sun. Tell me what is on that scroll."

"Nothing that little nightmares should worry about," Dominic pushed. Yes, he knew the different ways to travel, but there was a reason that Apocalypse Moon had been stuck with him until he made the deal with the Nightmare King.

It was almost impossible to escape him. As long as he wanted Dominic, he'd have him. He tried a couple of spells, but none of them worked. No incantation would work as long as he was near Nightmare King. His power cancelled out the rest. According to the scroll, there was only a couple of power sources stronger, but they were so strong, the way to summon them had been left out.

Knowing so many things, yet still unable to leave. He continued through his journey, doing what he could to warn the ones he needed to. However, time still went by. Dominic was fifteen and a half now. He'd been stuck inside that dank lair since he was thirteen. Thirteen years old with no memories of whom he had been.

"Is it time to let you go? Your stench is becoming more atrocious. Your rebelling attitude is hard to stand. What happened to the young boy that first came with such high hopes of reaching the lovers through their dreams?"

"You can't let me go until I reach Sera," Dominic reminded him. "Your stench is way worse though. No idea how any woman could put up with you. That dream faerie must be desperate for love."

"You are pushing it, boy!"

"Then send me where I need to go already, Mister Nightmare Man."

"You keep pushing and I will send you back to the little girl as a zombie!"

Nightmare King wouldn't let him go until he was sixteen, and Dominic knew it. He did have to stop pushing though. Frightening her as a zombie wouldn't be good. "Just send me back to her, at the proper age."

"Tell me what you have been hiding."

"A scroll that doesn't do me any good here." Dominic was honest, and he could just hear the pleasure of that ring in Nightmare King's voice.

"Good. As long as you realize that, boy."

CANDY MEETS HER LOP EARED BUNNY

"Welcome to Sweet Meats," Candy Sweet answered as she fumbled around for her notebook paper. "Can I take your order?"

"Yeah." One man at the table gestured to the other. "He and I want a sweet ham each."

"Okay, we will have that right out to you." Candy marked 2 h on her paper and headed into the kitchen where the magic happened. Not just the magic of good cooking though. She watched her sister Poured Sweet mixing some hamburger with her hands. Purple sparkles fell onto the meat. "Two Sweet H's."

"Go get the fresh kill because we are out on this side."

Ew. Candy moved away slowly. Sweet Meats used only the finest, freshest ingredients and that included the animals. They had a butcher that worked for them (thank goodness) but she would have to maneuver over there where there would be piles of dead animals still in their fur.

As Candy stepped in though, she changed her mind about retrieving the ham. In a cage with no butcher around was the world's largest and cuddliest bunny.

It was no ordinary bunny. It must have weighed twenty pounds. It was big and brown with large ears that dropped down instead of standing up straight. It had the tell-tell trait of a cottontail rabbit with the tuft on its rear end. The eyes weren't red but an enchanting emerald green and its black nose twitched.

She swore its eyes were pleading for her to help it. "Oh, you poor thing." She moved toward the cage and stroked its fur. "Got caught, didn't you?"

His sad eyes didn't let up. How could such a creature have such heart tugging eyes? She opened the latch and picked the big bunny up. Its hair was soft and cuddly, and it latched onto her like its life depended on it.

It was too much to bear. Holding it close, Candy headed away. She didn't get passed Poured though.

"Candy, what do you have there?" Her sister criticized her.

"Not this one. I won't do it again, just *not* this one." Candy rubbed the top of his head. "Come on, Poured, don't shout about it. Just look at his cute little floppy ear? He has a cotton tail too. How many rabbits are like that? Is that even possible to have both? He could be a new species. Oh, please don't tell."

Poured groaned. "Better get him out and then get back here. You also better pray no one orders rabbit while you are away. Bleeding heart."

Candy didn't care about the name calling. She marched over to the cleanest counter she could and sat the rabbit down. Luckily, it didn't pounce off from her. She took off her apron, grabbed her purse, and picked the gigantic rabbit back up. "I'll be right back, I promise, Poured."

Okay, so she didn't return back right away. Her new bunny after all needed something to eat. She stroked its ears as it munched on some carrots. "Doesn't take much to please you, does it? Look at you. Hopping around out there in the world with no care at all."

His eyes just stared back at hers as he finished munching on his carrot.

"Now that the butcher doesn't have you, it looks like your life just got better again. Well, sort of." Candy shrugged. "You are stuck with me until you run away. Not that I could blame you, big guy." She stepped away and took off her coat. "My life is far from uncomplicated, big bunny. My dad is dying in six months and my sister is already engaged to Stephen, a nonmagical user. To keep the business running, I have to marry this guy that is so . . ." She closed her eyes and groaned. "He just thinks of me and my competition as a sport. Dilly dallying, always acting like he doesn't know who to choose. I have to put up with it though." She moved back over toward the bunny and stroked his ears as his little mouth munched away on the carrot. "I'm a magic user, first class Sweet. I was even born in a traditional family line named Sweet. If I lose this company, then no one would hire me. I have none of those school credentials. I can read and write. I know mathematics extremely well. You have to in order to run the business. I am adept at the law and advertising statutes, but it's still not school. No credentials, no job. I can't remake a business without either one."

She moved away toward the window. "Yeah, you'll be hopping off soon, breaking out these windows I'm sure. Otherwise, you'll have to hear about my whining day after day. You've already been warned." She looked back and smiled at the bunny before heading to her room. "So, until you run away, what should I name you?" She closed the door and decided to change her clothes. It was warmer that day than the weatherman predicted.

As she threw her clothes on the bed, she heard a tiny foot repeatedly stomping in the other room. She opened the door and saw the bunny thumping it's foot. Oh, it was so cute! "Bunnies really do that?" She stepped closer. The bunny still hadn't left. "I haven't frightened you away yet, huh?" She watched, amazed, as he hopped all the way over to her.

He stood up on his haunches with his front paws in the air and Candy almost lost it. Did bunnies do that? Well, she knew that cats could. "You are too adorable for words!" She picked him back up and scratched the back of his ears.

She went to work once more, but was excited to return back home to her new bunny. Would it still be there when she returned? What should she do with it? Eventually she needed to take it back out to the wild where it belonged, but she was going to take her sweet time to do it.

In her life, it was about the only thing she felt was going right. When she returned home each night, he would always be there at the door to welcome her home. In the mornings, he would eat some vegetables she would buy for him the night before so that they were fresh. On the weekends when she could watch a movie, he always crawled up into her lap, and he let her stroke his ears. The first time he did that, it was quite a feat because she had taken him to the vet to get his health checked out.

Even after the trip, all he wanted was her. At night, she kept him at the foot of the bed, but by morning he had always sneaked into her arms, showering her with morning bunny kisses. He had a thousand chances to run away, but he never did, so Candy bought him a studded collar with the words BB on it. He was officially Big Bunny.

He was the best pet she could ever hope for. Then one day when she came back in an incredibly sour mood, he surprised her.

"I'm sorry, Candy."

Candy stared at him for more than a few seconds. He quickly tried to make his own rabbit mewling sounds, but it didn't cover it. "You talked?"

"I didn't mean to, but I couldn't help it." Big Bunny bent his head down on her lap. "That doesn't scare you, does it?"

"I have a bunny rabbit that talks?"

"I have a Candy that talks and I have no problem with it," Big Bunny joked. "I promise, I won't tell anyone your secrets. I'm just a talking rabbit."

"You've never talked before."

"I didn't want it to get awkward."

"You think?" Candy stroked his ears as he leaned into her hand. "Can all rabbits talk?"

"Some can, most don't," Big Bunny confessed. "Can I still curl up in your lap and live with you?"

"Well . . .you are still my Big Bunny, whether you talk or not." She scratched behind his ears. "I haven't been belittling you with petting, have I?"

"Oh no! I love being petted." He leaned into her hand again. "I wish you could pet me all day long, Candy."

"Okay." She looked at Big Bunny curiously. "Is there anything else you've been hiding from me?" Oh yes, she knew that little rabbit look.

"Nothing that you need to concern yourself with right now, Candy."

Heh. He probably ran away from the circus or something. That would make more sense. "Okay, keep your secrets." She kissed the top of his head. "Can I still give you bunny smooches?"

"Any time of day, Candy."

"Welcome to Sweet Meats," Candy Sweet answered as she fumbled around for her notebook paper again. "Can I take your order?"

"Yeah, two majbar pork slices, please."

"Okay, we will have that right out to you." Candy marked 2 p on her paper and headed into the kitchen "Two Sweet P's."

"Sweet Peas?" Her sister said as she looked back over at Candy. "I thought you weren't working the new veggie side yet."

"No, sweet pork." Candy forgot about the new addition again, it made their simple shortcuts harder sometimes when they sounded the same. "Po's, right?"

"No, that would be sweet potato," Poured answered. "Just stick with the full names, we'll figure it out."

Candy shrugged and set to work on her own order. Sweet hams and one meatloaf. She could cook and add the sweet, but then her mother would be left to it. Poured didn't have Spice power either, she had magical sprinklings for the hamburger, but she would have to wait for their mom too.

Their dad couldn't do it. The ability was only passed to the women of the family. That and he had been dying, barely getting out of bed now. A part of Candy felt bad but not much more than she felt for people who died on TV. He was the original one in the line, while her mom, Momma Sweet, had to pursue him. Her take was thirty percent which she split equally down with Candy and her sister. Each of them owned ten percent of the company, while the father she barely knew earned seventy percent without lifting a finger.

"Candy, take the veg side for two minutes. Table nine," her mother said as she rushed by her. "I am overflowing on the meat side. I swear; your father's idea of a veggie side is absurd. This will not keep the company going. Once he's dead, we need to change this."

Candy didn't speak to her mom about her similar thoughts. The veggie side was just taking up space and expenses. Cleaning her hands off, she grabbed her notepad and headed to the veggie side.

Cotton looked around the joint. This was not his kind of place, bad experience, but his friend Ryan had a crush on one of the waitresses there.

"I know what you are thinking," his friend Matt said, catching his eye roll. "Look, you can order majbar if you want."

"I've heard the name. What is it?"

"Majority is barbecue flavored."

Ugh. Why did everyone insist on doctoring food up? "Do they have donto?" Cotton asked.

"What is donto?"

"As in don't touch the food?" Cotton knew that annoyed him by the sound of his friend's sigh. "Majbab is better than anything else I guess." Smallest thing on the menu. He could then go home and get something decent to eat.

"My name is Candy Sweet, may I take your order?"

Cotton looked up at the waitress. His wailing about the place had ceased altogether as he stared at Candy. She never wore any makeup of any kind. Her hair was black and hanging down, the opposite of many women. The latest fashion was to put the hair up on the head, even young girls wore it like that. It wasn't a one day thing either, she always wore it like that.

Her dressing too. While she was covering up her outfit, it wasn't a waitress uniform. If she took off the apron, someone would swear she was some kind of business professional that just came in for a luncheon. That was actually a fantasy of hers she confessed one time to him.

If someone came in and said 'we'll take you without any scholing into our business', she wanted to rip off the apron and be ready to go. Candy was so brilliant, if only she wasn't stuck in family legacy. Family Business Personal Schooling didn't translate over into any other career path though. Sweet Meats may have been famous worldwide, but Candy would have been much better off if her family had let her get general education.

It was something banged into his mind every time she had a bad day.

She had brought out two decorative eggs. One with stripes. One with dots. Must have been on instinct or for decoration because he wasn't going to touch them.

"Is Poured working?" Matt asked the waitress.

"She's busy in the kitchen. I'm your waitress today," Candy answered as she fumbled through a notepad. "May I take your order?"

"Yeah, a majbar broccoli stew." Matt's voice lost interest. "My friend wants-"

"I can order for myself." Cotton handed his hand out to her, wishing she'd pick it up, but knowing better. If they were at home she would. She loved to pick him up at home. Then again, if she knew Big Bunny was actually him, she might not do that anymore. "Menu?"

"Oh." Candy groaned. "I don't really know the menu. I've never worked the veggie side before."

"You should." The words fell out before Cotton even comprehended them. "Do you have any regular food? Non-sweet or spicy?"

"That's a new request." Candy placed her notepad away. "You mean just get you something with nothing done to it?" She shrugged. "I don't see why not, but you'll have to pay something for it."

"That's fine. How about majbab price?" It was the only term Cotton knew. "Broccoli stew, we know it's on there."

"Okay." Candy marked down the item. "It's much cheaper to go to the market than eat here at Sweet Meats though for that, Sir."

"It'll be fine." He wasn't stingy with money.

"Okay, twenty nine, twenty nine."

"Pardon?" He wasn't stingy but he wasn't stupid. He looked toward Matt. "You're paying twenty-nine, twenty-nine for a simple stew?" All just so he could meet a girl who wasn't even waitressing right then?

"Sweet Meats adds no extra calories to the food, and we hold the top spot for sweetest barbecue in the world." Candy pulled the notepad back out. "One or two broccoli stews?"

"How about water?" Cotton asked. "Just bring some water."

"Five, twenty-nine."

"For water?" Cotton almost choked on the air.

"Sweetened or barbecue flavored water. Everything is sweetened or barbecue flavored." Her voice held great annoyance. "If you want regular, it's the same price, sir."

"Fine, whatever." Cotton gave up. She'd be in a better mood at home. "Get me a simple glass of water."

Candy turned to head back to get the orders, but she found herself stuck in a familiar embrace. Darren eagerly kissed her, giving her little room to complain. He was supposed to be marrying her after all. His breath wasn't the cleanest, but it never had been. Even barbecue would have been better than what she smelled. The customers could probably smell that.

When he let go of her, she tried to act like that wasn't completely embarrassing. "Darren, what are you doing here?"

"Counting the days until we get married." Darren looked over toward Cotton and the other guy. "You're not trying to flirt with my Candy, are you?" Neither of them bothered to answer, but Candy felt mortified. If anyone could get a reward for less tact, it would be him.

"What do you want, Darren?" Candy asked again, hoping she could find out so he could leave.

"The big day is getting closer. We'll be doing it soon." He grabbed her by the waist. "Marriage, of course."

Candy didn't want to look at anyone. What a display. Why did he have to be such a showoff? "I've got to go get an order."

"Hurry up then." He patted her butt before she headed on her way.

That had to be the biggest creep Cotton had ever seen. He'd heard of him several times. Who in the world comes in grabbing their fiancé like that? He'd seen romantic displays, but that was far from romantic. That smell on his breath too, he stank.

It wasn't right. Candy was the sweetest owner in the world. Well, part-time owner. He only spent his mornings, nights, and the weekends in his rabbit form. The other times he walked around like everyone else, doing his own thing.

He knew that he should have hopped off, but he had got rather close to her in his rabbit form. His family also reinforced him to stay, believing that they were both the prophesied ones. That large guy standing in front of him though, the thought of him always being near Candy sickened him. There would be no more curling up in her bed with that guy around. "Why does she have to marry you?" He knew the answer yet Cotton just couldn't help himself.

"Pardon?" The guy moved up closer, pounding his hands on the table. "What do you mean *why* does she have to marry me? Who are you?" Cotton moved back slightly, wincing at the awful breath. He heard him take a big sniff. Yeah, that's attractive. "You're a Vegan, what are you doing here?"

"I'm allowed." Cotton scratched his shoulder.

"Cotton, damn it, that's none of our business," Matt began. "Who cares who is marrying who?"

"Anyone would have to be blind to want to marry him after that showoff display." Cotton sat back in his chair. He shouldn't care. He should be going about his business complaining about the five, twenty nine water.

He remembered all those nights though, complaining about Darren Manner. She didn't want him in her life at all, and whether he wanted to say it out loud or not . . . Cotton wanted to be more than her pet. Not that that mattered, if she was the prophesied one then she would never have to worry about Darren Manner again.

"You need to watch that mouth of yours," Darren pointed at him. "I'm the guy who trademarked the currency signs. You should thank me when I let my wife use it for the menus around here in the future."

Yeah, this was the guy who actually got the dollar and cent signs trademarked. The reason they had to use commas for pricing now. He remembered the day Candy told him that fact.

"I always wanted to own the currency signs. I always own what I want, so don't cross me again."

Cotton kept himself under control. Just because he didn't have everything Darren had didn't mean he was a pushover.

Candy came back and sat the broccoli stew in front of Matt. It smelled weird, that spicy barbecue broccoli concoction. Candy then sat down his water. "Five, twenty nine, as agreed."

"Honey, you don't need to do that." Darren muttered closer to her ear. "Say five dollars and twenty nine cents. You'll get to say that every day soon."

Cotton couldn't help himself. "Showoff Spice man."

"Vegan."

"Boys." Candy chided between the two of them.

"Fine, I'll be good." Darren repicked up the water and sat it in front of Cotton. "Here."

Cotton held his hands up. "I would never touch anything you've touched."

"Oh, ouch." Darren knocked the water over. "Oops."

Cotton stared at the water on his shirt while Candy mopped up the mess on the table with a rag.

"Sorry, that's gratis. I'll get you another," she said. Turning she looked toward Darren. "Stop screwing with the customers, what do you want already?"

"I have some news." Darren crossed his arms. "Posh is coming over, and well, we need to discuss some things before she does."

"Posh? Posh Yum Num?" Cotton could hear the growl beneath Candy's words. "Why?"

POSH YUM NUM

"If it isn't little Candy," a voice called over before Candy could leave. A woman decked out in glitter sequins and showing off far too much skin strolled over to her like she owned the world. From that look and the way Candy looked at her, Cotton knew it was Candy's competition. Posh Yum Num.

"Posh." Candy held her ground against the other woman. "What are you doing here?"

"Letting you know that your family is about to fall." The woman breathed on her hand and showed Candy a pink sparkling cupcake ring. "I found the perfect Spice man. Sweet Meats is about to go down."

"Yum Num Cakes can't take down Sweet Meats." Candy shooed her away, missing the look on Darren. Cotton caught it though, and he knew things were about to get serious. "I'm working, I'll deal with you later."

"Your sister wants a husband that has no magic line at all."

"So?"

"So it's up to you, and last I looked, you're screwed."

Candy took a deep breath. "I already know who I'm marrying, okay?" She gestured toward Darren who politely coughed in his hand.

"Apparently, you don't." Posh laughed in her face as she shook her ring. "Marriage second, winner first."

Candy dropped her notepad. Her face was frozen with her eyes wide and her jaw completely dropped. "Darren?" She turned to look at Darren who had his hand on the back of his forehead.

"The penny drops." Posh danced around her a second. "Good luck looking for anyone else, he is the top man. He may have chosen you, but I'm so much more lovable. I am sweeter than Sweet. Like I said, pack it up. Soon it's all over, Yum Num Cakes will be number one."

Cotton looked down at his table. Oh no. That was going to hurt Candy. Her business would be doomed. She'd have to start at something brand new, from the beginning to gain experience. She was too late to start the schooling to advance. So much wasted potential.

"It's not too late," Candy sneered, her nose even getting wrinkly. "I'll find someone else. I've got a long time to find the right guy."

"You don't have to give up," Darren said to Candy. "Just give me some motive to change my mind. You're Sweet, so be sweet. I mean, you are supposed to be actually super sweet with sweet powers. You never dress sweet. I mean, look at that outfit under your uniform. What is up with the red business suits? That's not cute. You never speak cute in any way."

To him. Candy would never show Darren her sweet side. Meanwhile, Cotton had seen every side of her. Especially her cheery sweet side.

"You wish you could fool me," Candy Sweet" Posh prodded. "You think we don't know? Your dad is going to be dead soon." Posh snapped her finger at her. "The doctors predicted date, Yum Num is having a fifty percent off sale in celebration of it."

Cotton watched as others posing as customers grabbed Candy and held her back. Cotton jumped up along with Matt second. Things were getting out of hand.

"Stop right there." Cotton stood firmly in front of Posh with Matt at his side. Cotton always tried to play it safe. He played the recording of what she just said. "How many customers on the social will find that dead comment cute?"

Posh looked like she was ready to start a fight with him, but instead, Momma Sweet showed up.

"Candy Sweet is the sweetest woman alive, because like a sweet lady, she holds the sweetest secrets," Momma Sweet said. "Posh? What is your cute pet and how'd you get it?"

Posh just smiled. "I have the most adorable fluffy kitty that I got from a sweet old lady seller."

"Oh, is that all?" Momma Sweet gestured to Candy. "Darren? The woman you are letting go? Owns a 26 pound floppy eared cotton tail bunny rabbit, and she got it by saving it's life by stealing it from the butcher."

"Aww." A lot of the crowd agreed with Momma Sweet.

"Oh, that is sweet." Darren looked back at Candy. "What did you name it?"

Candy didn't look comfortable. "He's a big bunny, so I named him Big Bunny."

"The sweetest women don't have to flaunt or make up things to express how sweet they are," Momma Sweet told Darren. "They are naturally sweet, which is the best kind of sweet."

"Oh, I want to see your sweet bunny," Darren decided. "Naturally sweet? I never thought of it that way, what a dunce I am."

"Who cares about naturally sweet, look at her! She doesn't dress sweet or speak sweet or anything! Who cares what cute pet she has!" Posh snapped.

"I think there's a clear winner." Cotton moved closer to Candy's face. People sometimes were so mean, they had to force she had a pet rabbit out of her. She only told the people she wanted to know about him. Now that 'owning a bunny' news would be circling on the media? She never wanted him as a spotlight in anything. What he wouldn't give to be her Big Bunny right now so he-

Cotton felt himself getting shoved forward, his lips touching Candy's haphazardly.

Posh laughed as her crew began to leave Candy. "Guess what Candy? It doesn't matter how cute you are now. You just got kissed by a Vegan!"

Cotton had to admit, he didn't plan on Candy's mom dragging him around to the back. He tried to keep it together as they moved through the meat section. Piles of raw food in different sizes, piled up, bleeding and ew! How could people eat like that? He didn't say a word until he was yanked roughly in front of Momma Sweet with Candy coming up the rear side.

Her sweet face that always appeared on TV seemed to be gone. Everyone knew Momma Sweet, she was practically the brand's mascot.

"How dare Posh do such a thing!" Momma Sweet yelled. "Candy, this is bad."

Candy couldn't speak. She just pointed, harder and harder, drawing her hand back and forth. When she did finally speak, it only came out, "Vegan?"

Wow, what a crime? "Who cares if I'm vegan, vegetarian or whatever." That wasn't like Candy at all to be so judgmental. She needed to get it under control, it was just a kiss. Not even a good one, it was off balance and he barely met her lips. He had better bunny smooches with her than that one.

"You are only vegan by what you choose to eat? It's your choice?" Momma Sweet asked. "You don't have Vegan magic?"

Oh. "I don't know really." He never cared to know. It would make his chosen unable to taste sweet.

Candy gestured to Cotton again. "Posh knows Poppa Sweet is going downhill. She stole Darren Manner and she's wearing his ring. Now she's going to lie about this, isn't she?"

Momma Sweet's mouth dropped. "Why that no good wench! Those Yum Nums!" She grabbed Candy's hand. "Don't worry, whatever happened, Darren likes you more. You're kinder and prettier, a regular princess. Even though you don't dress like it, I intrigued him with your bunny. It doesn't matter the rumors, he saw what she did in person. We can work this out. We have to work this out." Momma Sweet held her daughter's face. "Your sister's already marrying someone from a normal line, and the Yum Nums will start rumors now about Vegan magic. Poppa Sweet is almost gone, Candy, what are we going to do to keep Darren Spice?"

Momma Sweet turned to look at Cotton. "Sir? What's your name?"

"Cotton?" Shoot, now wasn't the time for 'Tail'. "Just, Cotton's fine," he said.

"Cotton. Please, let me discuss some things with my daughter. Go sit down and Candy will meet you later."

MOMMA SWEET ISN'T SO SWEET

"You know what is next, Candy," her mother warned her as she unwrapped a piece of chocolate and popped it in her mouth. Candy spit it out fast. It tasted disgusting. "It's already begun. You know what must be done."

"I can't," Candy said as she grabbed her head, "it's crazy." She knew what her mom was about to say.

"Cotton is a Vegan. He stole your Sweet power. Right now, you cannot taste sweet. That will change, and soon you will have no Sweet power. The only way to save your Sweet power, is to dominate the Vegan power. To dominate, you must kiss Darren."

"If I bend to that, then I will have nothing left to hold over Posh to make him marry me still."

"Which is why you need to be with the Vegan, but make Darren jealous."

"But the business-"

"Make that Cotton guy think you are his girlfriend, *but* marry Darren." Momma Sweet shrugged. "Darren is like Poppa Sweet, he likes to fool around the same way. Seeing you with not only a different boyfriend, but someone who annoyed him too, should make him pine for you even more. Cotton never backed down from him, I saw that."

"Momma . . ." Candy fidgeted with her fingers. "Is there no other option? I don't want to lead anyone on."

"I know you don't, you really are a sweet person. But? You cannot live in limbo. Sweet and Vegan do not mix haphazardly. You know that you will lose more than just your Sweet power."

"We'll lose the business." It was a question that Momma did not need to answer. "What is it exactly you want me to do?" Knowing Darren, she knew her mother had been right. Those were her only options. After her mom gave her the few options she had, she stood up and she went to go clean on the veggie side before she confronted Cotton.

"It's okay." Momma Sweet turned to her daughter Poured as they continued to fix chairs into the night. "The whole plan has moved smoothly so far."

"I know. I didn't bother telling Darren everything, so it's risky. He sure didn't mind the Posh part," her daughter Poured Sweet said, pushing in the last chair. "Candy is going to hate this, mom."

"Candy will have to understand. If the business collapses, she'll have a hard life. If the world ends though?" Momma touched Poured's hand. "No one will have a life. She will understand, have faith in that. We must do this."

"I know. It's the best thing. For the business, for the world, and for everyone." Poured grabbed the broom and swept up the ground. "I feel bad for the guy though. This is sick what we have to do. Plus, Darren? He's kind of scummy, but this isn't going to be nice to him either."

"He has free will, nothing bad is happening to him." It wasn't nice but there wasn't a choice. Posh ending up with Darren was Momma Sweet's plan. Posh pushing Candy into Cotton wasn't her idea but she noticed fate. Eventually, Darren would come back and take Candy's hand in marriage.

But before then, she needed to be in love with Cotton Tail.

Their prophecy of the end of the world was just as mysterious as anything else. Momma Sweet never thought about it when she named her second born Candy. There had been many Candy's in the family line. She never thought about it until at the age of five, Candy woke up one night screaming for her.

//"Momma!"

Momma Sweet moved to her daughter's room. It was two o' clock in the morning and her little Candy was crying for her. When she came to her room, Candy's hands were rubbing her eyes. Momma Sweet sat down next to her on the bed. "What is it, Candy? Did you have a bad dream again?" She expected to hear her daughter talk about a monster under the bed, or maybe something in the closet. Instead, she heard something that she would never forget.

"I dreamed of the apocalypse and these people that weren't people, mommy. Their skin was flaky and their eyes were light blue. They wanted me. I ran but then a dragon flew over my head and these miniature bodies were falling on me like rain. I called for you over and over, but the ground and everything faded away and I was trapped in blackness!" She grabbed onto her mommy's shoulder.

Apocalypse? She was five, how could she even know that word? Those visions. Momma Sweet held onto her tightly. "Candy, where did you hear that word from?"

"A boy. He tried to say something, but I ran away from him. I don't like boys, they have cooties, and Michael has the most cooties. Michael always chased me on the playground, and he was chasing me in my dream. He chased me and I told him to stop it and he didn't and so he ran and he chased and then all that stuff happened."

Momma Sweet swallowed but held her daughter tight. That was no ordinary dream. For as long as time had been, the world had a prophecy that one day healthy and sweet would meet. The terms were very prophetic and not easy to understand. In fact, it was an entire book which hardly had any complete sentences. Yet, it was the oldest book on the planet, and no one knew how it ever existed or who wrote it. The most their ancestors could make of it was that one day someone from a pure Sweet line named Candy would fall for a Vegan named Cotton Tail. As her daughter began to cry, all the strange lines came crashing back to her.

Candy was supposed to end up with a Vegan to save the world. However, she was Momma Sweet's only daughter. They held a magic business called Sweet Meats, and if Candy married herself to a Vegan? She would never get the Spice power she needed to run the business.

Momma Sweet would need to have one more daughter, and pray that she found someone who held the magic of Spice. Spice and Sweet created the sweet and savory barbecue business that had been running their family line for over two hundred years.

There was no way to sell a magic business. If it went kaput, it was the end. "It's okay, Candy, it was just a dream. Go back to bed, Sweetie." She tucked her daughter back in, calmed her down some more until she was ready to go to sleep, and left the room.

She would have to tell Marlen they had to have one more child for the business.

For without the business, they would lose everything. The houses, the cars, and the traditional fame of the Sweet family. He would have to agree. Otherwise, Momma Sweet didn't want to imagine the choice she'd have to make against her little Candy.//

Candy wiped the back tables on the veggie side. Matt had left, and only Cotton was in the restaurant. Her mom and sister were back on the restaurant's meat side, straightening it up she presumed. It was night and the doors should have been locked, but Cotton and her still needed to have a big talk. A real big talk. She wiped down the table for the last time. They were starting to shine having been cleaned over and over just to ignore the talk, but she couldn't stop the inevitable. Knowing that she'd have Big Bunny's comfort when she went home, she headed over toward Cotton's booth. She sat down on the other side and tapped her fingers on the table. "What do you want to do?"

Cotton lifted his eyes toward her. She hadn't noticed before, but he had a beautiful set of emerald eyes like her rabbit. Hopefully that was a good sign. He unfolded his arms and relaxed his body. "What is the big problem?"

He was joking, right? No one grew up without knowing this basic information. Candy tapped the table again. "Twenty to thirty days I need to have this resolved."

"Twenty to thirty days. Okay." Cotton nodded. "Let's get out of this place, get to know each other, and you can give me the specifics." Cotton held his hand out to her for a handshake. "Deal?"

"Get to know each other?" That wasn't the best idea. "I'm getting married eventually to Darren. I mean, well, I should. Somehow. I'll get past Posh."

"You are going to be begging and pleading for him to take you back?" Cotton rolled his eyes.

Judgmental. Candy stuck her tongue in her cheek. "He's not much different than my dad was with my mom. It's the way things are with Spice men usually."

"So Spice pushes Sweet around?"

"Nobody pushes me around." Candy moved further away from him in the booth, preferring the far end. "My dad is dying soon. Our business is about to fold. I have no one to take care of me, and at my mother's age she'll be taken away. I have no authority to start another business. My sister will be on thin ice herself. Most of all? I don't really care for anyone. If I don't *love* anyone, and everything is about to be taken away, what would you do? I need to preserve the business first."

"You could go out and get a regular job."

"I've never done anything else. I've been groomed since birth to take over the business." Candy wasn't going to give into that. "I don't have any of the certifications children received when they were younger." She expected him to ask about certifications or equality tests, but he didn't.

"Okay then, let's go out." Cotton stood up. "Do you need a jacket?"

"Out." Candy slid out of the booth. "Fine. The sooner we get this over with, the sooner I can go back after Darren."

"Well that's great 'cause I hate that guy. Postponing him makes me happy." Cotton headed to the front door. "Besides, you should enjoy this too."

She should enjoy this? "Why should I enjoy this?"

"A chance to make him jealous?" Cotton looked back at her, straight into her eyes. He kept staring uncomfortably. "There isn't an ounce of jealousy in your eyes."

"Business."

"Have you ever dated anyone except that guy?"

No, of course not. She needed to stay free for Darren. Only Poured dated around when she was younger, and she was exclusively taken now.

"Well, come on, I'm hungry." Cotton held the front door open. "Your overpriced water on my shirt wasn't fulfilling."

"I don't know." Candy fidgeted. "I have a pet at home, I should really get back to him."

"It is just a pet."

"Big Bunny is not just a pet, he is *my* pet." Candy sighed. "Never mind, you would never understand. "

"One drink. You'll be back to your little guy before you know it."

"Fine. Where are we going then?"

"You'll see."

C andy sat down on the unfamiliar barstool in front of the metal counter.

"Hey, Kit." Cotton slapped his hand against the waiters. "Two broccoli stews." He gestured toward Candy. "She's never had the real thing."

"Coming up." Kit moved away from Candy's sight. She turned to look at the scenery. The smells were different than anything she'd ever smelled before. Her nose must have been changing too. "Unfamiliar world," she muttered softly not thinking anyone would hear.

"Exciting new world," Cotton said from beside her. She lifted her eyes to his. "Give it a try, Candy. You already know what your future is supposed to be, always have. What's it hurt to try something new?"

Candy didn't respond to his question because she didn't know how to. He wasn't even supposed to hear her. How did he have such good hearing? She rubbed her face. "Cotton. You said you wanted to get to know each other, so tell me something about yourself already."

"Well for one, I think your mom is kind of freaky."

What? Instead of talking about himself he just dissed her mother? "Are you sure you date often? Insulting mothers isn't first date talk."

Cotton laughed. "No, probably isn't. I don't know, it's a date, but not." He shrugged. "Unlike a real date, I'm not looking to impress you. I mean, I don't even know what you wanted to talk to me about."

"You do not? Are you really that clueless?" Candy felt her temperature rise. This guy just wanted to tease her for the month before he finally took what he wanted. It would be a long month.

"Oh." Cotton winced. "This is something basic I should know, isn't it? I'm not stringing you along to be mean."

Why was he really doing this? "Is there any remote chance you'd choose to marry me within a month?"

Cotton just shot a surprised look her way as the broccoli stews arrived. "What?"

Candy looked at her broccoli stew. It was nothing she had ever tried before; he'd been right about that. "I'd pay you. I make okay money, and once I secure the business, I could pay a whole lot more?"

Cotton picked at his stew. "I am confused. I don't want to jump into anything with someone I don't even know."

"It doesn't have to be real. It's? I need Darren Manners, and because of that kiss, Posh will stir up rumors that will ruin the business. Darren doesn't care about rumors, he cares about cute and sweet and his property. If I act cute and sweet, and you have me as yours instead? He might turn before the month is over."

Cotton just looked at her very weird. "I know you really want your business. There's another future waiting out there for you." He glanced at her. "You think he'd really fall for it?"

"He wants to see my bunny," she groaned. "I'll be the sweetest and cutest thing I can on like a double date. With, Posh. I'll concede, act like I accepted you so I'm not . . ." She fidgeted her fingers. "Starving on the streets. I know, it's stupid, I will make it up to you if you decide to help. I'll take this to go." Candy gestured toward the food. "Come by Sweet Meats tomorrow please? We both need a good night to sleep on this."

"Ooooh!" Candy whined as soon as she came through her door. Cotton had beat her home, becoming her beloved Big Bunny. He was right in front of the door waiting for her. She put down a grocery bag so she could pick him up instead. "Big Bunny, I had the worst day of my life so far!"

Cotton enjoyed her caresses as she moved toward the window with him. He knew what her day would be all about.

"I lost Darren Manner." Candy lied him on his fluffy pet bed next to the window. "Posh stole him, and then she made me kiss a stranger! She's going to come up with all kinds of lies, and the whole city will believe her because she's so sweet and innocent to them. To top it off, I can't taste sweet anymore for at least a month, and that's if he doesn't have Vegan power. I have nothing to impress Darren with except you." She patted his furry ears as she cried. "Momma Sweet wants me to use jealousy to win Darren. She thinks pretending that I will give up and marry this guy Cotton, then being super cute as much as possible will win him back. I'm even willing to pay what I can. Do I have the words 'take advantage of me' written somewhere?" She checked her clothes.

"Lose your sweet taste?" Big Bunny didn't know that. "I guess you'd never even consider someone who wasn't Sweet or Spicy then?"

"Hm? No," Candy said, "I'd be open to it. It's just a month after all with a nonmagical user. As long as they didn't try to convert me, then I wouldn't mind." She nestled his floppy ears with her nose. "After all, I love my Big Bunny."

Big Bunny rubbed noses with her. "Yeah? What about someone that had Vegan power? Would you ever give them a chance?"

"Well? I mean." She blushed. "If Cotton helps, I'm going to make up a story that he has ties to a Vegan company. It'll make my move to Cotton make more suitable sense to Darren. I wouldn't be able to ever taste Sweet, but then I could make vegetables taste like they were fresh no matter how long ago they were picked."

Big Bunny sighed and wiggled his nose. That was the business side of her talking. "I mean, would you really date someone with that power?"

"Oh." Candy didn't look as good. "I don't really ever have to think about that. It hurts to ever think there is a choice." She patted the back of his neck softly. "I would choose to lose whichever flavor I had to, forever, if it meant being with someone I really cared for." She scratched her arm and bit her lip.

Shoot, he had made her sad with his question. "What does this guy Cotton have to do to make you feel better?"

"Just play pretend, but it's still going to cost big, Big Bunny." Candy patted him again. ""If he doesn't play his part, I'm in real trouble." Candy lifted his floppy ears and they drooped back down to his sides. "I may not be able to take care of you anymore, Big Bunny. If I have to, I will have to drive you out far away from the city though so you don't end up anywhere near a menu."

Losing Candy's physical presence? Ever since the day he'd almost been gutted and killed like an ordinary rabbit, she had been his light. Mere minutes away. He got stuck in a cage on his way home, and he had wasted too much power, making him incapable of changing back to a human on that day. When she stole him away, talked to him, and caressed his floppy ears, he couldn't leave her. Now, she would be taken away if he didn't do *something*. He hated that she needed him to play as Cotton for this charade, but himself as Big Bunny couldn't waste anymore time.

"Everything's changing." Candy gestured to her front door. "I went out to get ice cream and a cake to make myself feel better. Then I remembered halfway home what I was doing." She rested her head on the window. "They are just souvenirs now." She looked toward him. "Anyhow, you must be hungry." She slid away from the window and moved back toward the bags. "I have to try this broccoli stew. The other guy, Cotton, he got it for me. At least he's halfway nice." She sighed. "Probably not a good thing though. The last thing I need is to get to know some guy and then have to marry Darren. It's just twisting the knife, you know?" She shook her head. "I don't even know his last name yet."

"I know, Candy." There was only one real choice. It was time to act soon. "After a good night's sleep, you'll know what to do." Ever since Big Bunny met her, he knew how she felt about never having control of her life. Well, it was time to let her be in control. She would know the truth, and make her own decision.

All they had was a name in the prophecy, but that was going to have to be enough because he had to try.

One more night as her big, fluffy Big Bunny. When she came to bed, after finally eating the broccoli stew, he nudged against her. Putting down her spoon, she scratched his ears.

One more night.

Candy felt Big Bunny's presence beside her, but she felt something else as well. Opening her eyes, she saw a figure.

"Candy Sweet," it spoke beside her bed. She had no idea who this person had been. "I visited you once in a different form. Do you remember me?"

"What a strange dream. If I am dreaming of a regular guy, then why not dream of someone cuter?" She wiggled her hands as she yawned. "Well, semi-cute. You'll grow into it." The figure's cheeks blushed.

"I'm here to tell you about the apocalypse—"

"Apocalypse? Man, that broccoli stew really messed me up, didn't it?" She yawned again, but the figure disappeared.

She opened her eyes and saw her rabbit cuddling up beneath her chin, thumping his little feet. "Running from prey? I know how you feel." She snuggled her head back into the pillow, ready to finish her rest. As the night went by, she forgot all about the dream.

APOCALYPSE MAN

"It didn't count," Dominic reasoned with himself as he felt his abrupt return. "It didn't count, she didn't call me a man. It was just an expression."

"It was foretold."

Dominic glared into the darkness again. It didn't count. Apocalypse Moon wouldn't do anything that would make him feel such contempt. It was impossible. What could the only person he knew ever do to become an enemy? Would he be seeing her messing with destined lovers perhaps? That would frustrate him, but it would not make her his enemy in his heart. "It was nothing. I-I should go back."

"I think not. I feel it's time. You know it's time."

HOPPING ALONG THE BUNNY TRAIL

Candy wiped down the counters, watching the door. She stayed on the veggie side today, wondering when Cotton would come in already. She heard the front door open, but didn't see anyone. She figured it was a patron of Sweet Meats that quickly realized they were on the wrong side. Hardly anyone wanted to eat on the veggie side. Not when there were way better restaurants made for them.

Spice, Sweet and Vegan. Candy hated that they were even trying this, it felt like it was grasping, but it didn't economically make sense. They had to pay more for fresh vegetables and they had to throw it out fast. They hardly had people coming in, and when they do they get slapped with the high prices of Sweet Meats.

If Candy was in charge, she probably would add something small to the menu. Something special, one thing that other places didn't have. After seeing that progress, she would add more and get people who already used Sweet Meats to add the new pieces into their repertoire. Oh, or maybe they could add something small to the end of the meal for free that was a veggie? Then, maybe hiring out for an actual Vegan power for that veggie would-?

-she felt a familiar furry feeling beside her leg. Looking down she saw Big Bunny. "Big Bunny?" How in the world did he get there?

"You silly boy, what are you doing all the way out here?" He must have followed her to work. Maybe he had caught a ride in her purse? Well, either way, it was too dangerous for her bunny rabbit to be out at Sweet Meats. When she went down to pick him up though, something happened.

Big Bunny quickly hopped away with her disoriented and falling asleep. He needed to keep her asleep. Seeing him in his human form would complicate things and he didn't want her to see him change into Cotton. Still, he felt bad about how he had to accomplish his goal and soothed her while she slept. "It's okay, Candy. I would never hurt you." He patted her left ear softly, they were now as large as his own rabbit form's had been. He quickly headed out the front door and placed her in his truck.

Shutting the door, he quickly took off. He had already used his magic to make sure she didn't wake up. What he said was more for his benefit considering she'd never hear it. "I know that wasn't what you were expecting. Telling you what I have to, isn't going to be easy."

Candy lied unconscious in her own dreamland. Her fur was a soft white with streaks of blonde, and she had the cutest cotton tail he'd ever seen. Her ears flopped over like his, the tell-tale trait of a cottontail and lop eared rabbit.

Cotton kept his eyes on the road though. "Most times I can change forms, but that day you saved me? I couldn't because I had spent too much of my power. I know I should have left afterwards, but you were kind to me. I did make a good pet too, didn't I? I did share that I could talk, it wasn't completely dishonest, was it?" He stopped though when he saw it had started to snow. Weather used to be more predictable. Those days though, snow even happened in the dead of spring. It made things worse on his family.

Today the snow was really getting out of control. He could already see it piling up on the sides. It would be cold where they were going. He headed out of town up into Bunny Hills. He drove to the top before opening the door. He changed back into his original appearance as a bunny rabbit and took the sleeping spell off of Candy.

Candy backed up even further, tumbling down below the front seat under the dashboard.

"Candy." Candy tried to hop back up on the front seat, but she only managed to hop a little on her back paws. Cotton jumped down to her and gestured toward the opened door. "Don't run away, this is temporary. When it's finished, you'll still have a big choice up in the air." Cotton jumped down first. He knew the car was a little high but Candy would need to jump at some point. It's what rabbits did. "Come on, Candy."

Candy made a small squeak and jumped down. "You drove a car, Big Bunny?"

"Yes." He hopped away slightly, trying to get her to follow. "I have to warn you, my family and our business is unique. Come on."

Candy didn't budge though. "My Big Bunny? Drove a truck?"

Cotton hopped over to her. "I'm more than a bunny. I know everything about you."

"That's because I shared everything with my bunny." She tried to move back, but hopping backward wasn't easy. "You said you talked, but you never said that you could drive too. How did you drive?"

"Candy, I'll explain later." Candy was still far from cheerful, but Cotton couldn't stay out there that long. It was freezing. "Come on. It's high time I show you my home."

Her Big Bunny. Her talking Big Bunny had turned her into a bunny rabbit. It was strange enough dealing with her sweet big guy when she knew he could talk and communicate with her. But this?

Okay. She had to keep her head on her shoulders, follow Big Bunny, and get through this. She hopped over to a hole along with him. A deep, dark hole. He hopped in like it was nothing.

Yeah, no, sure. Who didn't live in a hole in the ground? Okay, she wouldn't whine. She hopped in slowly, hoping nothing came out to try and bite her. They traveled down into the hole farther until she saw light at the end of the tunnel.

When she came out, she was stunned. It was a room full of rabbits working on a conveyor belt. Out popped radishes, celery, carrots, and veggies of every kind.

"This way." Big Bunny poked at her butt with his nose. She looked back at him unkindly. He may be used to that, but no one poked her butt like that. "Come on, don't be timid."

"I'm not."

Big Bunny just hopped past her. "This way, Candy. I will take you somewhere more comfortable."

Big Bunny led her straight through some large pathways. "This is home so far. It's warmer down here, but there's not much sun. You can go to the surface, but the special amenities you are used to aren't here."

Yes, including bathrooms or being human. She figured that out quickly. Candy scratched her head. Well, tried to more like it. "It's different." *Real* different. "Okay, you live down a rabbit's hole and conduct some sort of veggie business?"

"Sort of."

"Candy!"

Candy heard her name and watched a woman hop over to her. "Candy of legend!"

Candy of legend? Candy looked over at Big Bunny. "What does she mean?"

"Oh, it is an old saying. Our purpose here is unclear," Big Bunny said. "A sweet person named Candy is supposed to help us find our purpose again to save everything."

"Is that why you stayed and kidnapped me?"

"Kidnap is such a strong term," Big Bunny said as he used his hind leg to scratch his side. "Thats my mom you are talking to."

"Not complete though," his mother added. Her foreign accent and incorrect grammar was heavy, but Candy couldn't place it. "Found Candy in accident. Once we put names together, we figured out."

Unbelievable. Not only was Candy stuck in the hardest month of her life, she was expected to save some other business?

"It is another option," Big Bunny reminded her. "Instead of Sweet Meats, you could do something else with your life."

There was nothing else beside Sweet Meats. "I'll help get your business back together, but after that, you are on your own." She was a pro at business, had several sessions with the best there had been, and had top notch teachers hand-picked for her.

She would save Big Bunny. Herself though? It would be a fifty-fifty chance.

Still, it was better than having to release him out in the wild again.

Candy realized that Big Bunny's situation was *extremely* different as he opened the door to the next room.

Chicks. Hens. Ducks. All of them about the size of her bunny. All around them were eggs. Several hundreds of thousands of eggs. They were normal sized eggs, but there was such a massive amount of them. "What is with all the eggs?"

"When a hen likes a rooster . . ." Big Bunny waved a hand through the air.

"Okay, but why so many eggs?"

"My kind does not like eggs."

"Vegan? I thought unfertilized eggs were okay."

Big Bunny chuckled. "Candy, if you have not guessed yet, we are vegan, but we aren't really Vegan. We are not from your world." He gestured to her. "But, you are connected to us. The regular people with no power were born in this dimension. What you call Sweet, Vegan and Spice users were not meant to be here. Your great ancestors are our great ancestors, and you simply mixed into this world."

"You mean, magic users were not originally from here?" Candy asked. "Then what was I?"

Big Bunny gestured to the chicks coming over to cuddle. "The saying 'as sweet as a baby chick,' is half right. You'd be a hen. Maybe a duck."

"Vegans are descended from rabbits," his mother added, "and Spices are-"

"Wolves." Big Bunny growled. "I hate Spice."

"No son, love all."

Hen. Candy would be a hen. "I would be a hen?"

"Like human is all so important?" A hen nearby her squawked.

"Be nice," Big Bunny said to the hen. "Candy is what your great descendants will be like."

The hen didn't say anything else.

Neither did Candy.

THE EASTER BUNNY AND CANDY OF LEGEND

"We don't know what world we came from originally. Other worlds gave my ancestor's names," Big Bunny began. "The most familiar was Easter Bunny."

"Easter Bunny?"

"Yes. It doesn't matter what it was called though, my ancestors all did their part. We hand out baskets to good children. We travel from dimension to dimension, doing this simple deed." He looked back toward her. "It worked fine here when we came, at first, but then things got rocky. Our special baskets became ho-hum gifts people called fruit baskets. It doesn't matter what kind of magic we have paired with it."

"Husband gone, six years," his mother said, trying to communicate to Candy again. "World cruel. No hire without certify."

"Oh, I know that firsthand." Candy nodded, understanding enough of her broken language.

"We mostly live on veggies, so it wasn't that hard to adapt," Big Bunny said, "but life could be so much better if we had our purpose back."

A fruit basket. They were known for a fruit basket. Candy rubbed her head, wondering how a fruit basket could ever seem magical. "How was it magical?"

"We have powers to distribute easily." He waved his hand and blue sparkles came from it. "Children would wake up and see a special basket just for them."

"This was your business? Nonprofit, or was there some profit? How do you fund it?"

"With our bare hands. With our bare magic."

"Okay, then obvious question." Candy threw her hands up in the air. "Why?"

"Well . . ." He paused. "Candy, our kind, we have been moved around several different dimensions. Our original world held many more like us. This world is not our first try."

"For what?"

"Magic. Do you not get it?" Big Bunny asked. "The *mystery* of magic makes the dimensions tick. Every time more magic is lost, more must be made up for it. It was my ancient great grandfather that chose special baskets for good children. Because children? They believe in the impossible."

"So you have been to multiple dimensions?"

"Yes, to try and save them."

"Magic and faith stop apocalypse," his mother added as glittery waves of magic sprang from her paws in the form of a rainbow. "We try."

"So magic bunnies want me to save their business, that is nonprofit, to save my dimension from an apocalypse?" Candy really tried not to laugh. "Big Bunny, have you seen any signs at all that the end is coming? Fire? Brimstone?"

"We pick a special time to distribute baskets because it is the last time to become affected." He sighed. "Have you noticed snow outside? It's Spring."

Candy had noticed of course. "It is not a big deal."

"How much did it snow when you were a little girl?"

"Only in Winter."

"And now?"

"So you mean the snow is the sign?"

"We have seen so much worse," he said taking Candy's hand. "It may seem ridiculous to you, but to us, it is important. If we do not figure out how to add the mystery of magic back to this world? It will be gone. This may be the last magic basket day. We may have to leave before it's too late."

"But this world does have magic."

"You have formulas. You have restaurants. Your magic does not act like magic anymore. There is no mystery to solve. Candy, your ancestors were designed to use that magic in a different way. The way you use it now, it will not stop anything."

"Children must believe," Big Bunny's mother said. "No matter what adults say to explain. Children *must* believe in the unexplained. Do you understand?"

It was a hard thing to understand. Magic baskets saved everything? "My ancestors were like you, but you have moved through different dimensions. So, are you coming back around to this dimension?"

"Some of us settle in a dimension, and don't leave. Yes, we are circling around. It has gotten that bad, Candy. Selfishly, we want to at least try to save our descendants."

Because no one else can. A part of Candy wanted to laugh at the impossible notion. However, she had raised a rabbit who talked. She watched a hen cluck at her. She met Big Bunny's mom who hopped better than walked.

So... "Take me to your production line." It didn't change her plans. She wanted to help Big Bunny and she would.

Candy stared at the basket in front of her. Nothing seemed magical about it. Regular fruit was not going to seem magical. Candy grabbed one of the berries. She would not have the ability long, but if she got them on the right foot, they could figure out a solution next year.

She breathed and rolled until the berry had changed into what would taste like a delicious piece of candy. She placed it back into the basket. "Children are the secret? Children love candy."

"Candy?" Big Bunny did not sound so sure. "Candy rots teeth."

"Not my candy," she reminded him. "You said we were from the same line. Maybe this is why we have it."

"I have never been fond of candy."

"You're a rabbit, you want your veggies, but I do not know many children that would turn down candy."

"Might be right." His mother shook her head.

"It is not bad for them," Candy reminded Big Bunny. "No more than the veggies are. Not with my magic." She poked at the basket. "Are all of these brown? You could really use color, children love colors."

"We don't have a tie-dye basket machine."

"Well you need color." Candy continued to change the fruit into sweet fruit.

"Should we put a note that says children can eat as much as they want?" Big Bunny asked.

"Oh no, never. Children crave bad stuff. Tell them it is good for them, and they might not like it as much. Psychology." Candy looked around again but Big Bunny's mother was gone. She was alone with him. "Did I say something wrong?"

"You are changing everything, but we must trust you. I think mother is having a harder time with your new thoughts." Big Bunny shrugged. "You have weird thoughts."

They were only weird to a bunny rabbit. "I am trying to help."

"Legend foretold that Candy would make vast changes." He rolled his eyes. "I thought it was just your name."

"You know," Candy said, "our world had a prophecy too. So many were named Candy though. I don't know if I am the right one." She looked over at Big Bunny. "But I have to take care of you. Apocalypse or not, you are my Big Bunny."

"I know." He didn't sound thrilled with her statement. "I am still just your pet bunny."

The eggs. The fruit. How did they keep them? So many eggs. Fruit during the snow? They obviously couldn't go to the store, they had no money. "Big Bunny?" He looked back at Candy. "You never explained about the eggs. None of them smelled."

"The hens and ducks have the power to keep their eggs fresh forever. That way, if there is a chick, it stands the most likely chance of survival without sitting on it all day."

"Hm. I like my power better," Candy smiled at him. "Not that it helps you personally. Speaking of personal, I have my own problems at home."

"I know, Darren. I did not forget. We are heading on our way out right now." Big Bunny looked back at her. "Will you come again?"

"Maybe, but I have to go back home for now." It was easier said than done. The snow covered the hole. Big Bunny dug with his little paws, and even Candy helped.

"The snow is too intense."

"How can there be a blizzard in the middle of spring?"

"You already know the answer," Big Bunny reminded her. "You are stuck here until morning. After that, I will take you back."

"Is there enough room?"

"Sure. As there has always been room for me in your bed, I can share mine."

Candy had expected his room to be a small room big enough for a rabbit, but it was large. It wasn't a bed like hers, but gigantic bedding made of multiple pillows and large blankets. "This is your room?"

"Yes. I thought the snow might make things hard to make it back home." He raised his eyes toward her. "You accepted me when you found out I talked. Will you still accept me through all this?"

"Your pet status is in serious question." Once again, he didn't like the words though. "Changing things with Darren. Changing things with you."

"I am still the one that makes you feel better. I'm the one you talk to when life gets rough," Big Bunny reminded her. "I'm the one who curled up next to the bed with you." He made a strange sound from his throat. "Not that *wolf*."

"Oh, do we have to go there?" She did not want to have that discussion. "I have to work it out with Darren."

"If this worked, you could just stay here instead with us." Big Bunny touched her head and patted it. "No messing with the wolf anymore."

"What do you mean if it worked?"

"If the baskets idea worked, you could be here using your magic every year."

"But my magic is limited." Did he not get that at all? "I don't know how it happens with you, but I know how it happens with my kind. I have to get that kiss out of me or it'll fade soon."

"I have bunny smooched you several times," he reminded her. "You've never had problems with your magic before."

"I never had a problem with my taste before either. You are different, great for you. I am not and things are different." Candy just wanted to go to sleep. Curl up and just go to sleep.

"How?"

"It's so elementary for my kind." Candy crawled into bed. "I have to give kiss the wolf to undo the damage." There, that was one way to put it. Unfortunately, Big Bunny didn't let that stand. He lifted the sheets off of her.

"Excuse me? What do you mean you have to kiss the wolf?" His eyes. Now he had those real red rabbit eyes for just a few seconds before they moved to his emerald green. "Candy, you had better talk to me. You didn't talk to me last night either and you always do."

Candy tried to pull the covers back up, but he stopped her again. He wasn't going to give in. "I'm not like you. My magic is different." She slowly met his eyes. "I can't ask that strange Cotton guy, so the wolf will have to work."

Candy felt him get under the blankets. He petted her head much like she did him and he gave her a bunny smooch on the top of her forehead.

"That is wrong. No way are you going to kiss that wolf."

"Damn it, Big Bunny, what do you want from me?" She tried to make him stop petting her head, but she couldn't. She had to admit, she enjoyed it. Still. "The wolf is how I'm going to have to make it to help you."

"No way. You haven't worked this long to have to do that. I don't care if you hate my home and want Sweet Meats. That's fine, but you won't end up that way. I swear it, Candy Sweet."

Cotton adjusted his bowtie before he knocked on the door. He should not be happy about the situation but there was a lighter skip to his step. Candy did not know that her bunny was Cotton. If she did, she would probably freak out. So far, Candy had kept herself in control well, but this might be too much for his little magic user. She needed to see another side of him. Something besides the 'pet' she confided in and held all the time. If she had feelings for him as Cotton, then maybe she would not go after the wolf's kiss. She would stay with him. Not as an owner, but as something more.

He'd had feelings for Candy almost the moment his nose twitched in her direction. All she had was a need to help his adorable butt out.

Even with the magic baskets, she was helping him because he was her pet. There was a good chance she didn't even believe in the apocalypse, she was just doing her duty as a good owner. Making sure he was taken care of after everything fell on her.

Well, it didn't matter how underhanded it may feel, the ends justified the means. Cotton was now an option, there was *more* than Darren.

And there was no way that wolf was laying a paw on Candy.

Cotton held the white lilies in his arms presentably as he knocked on the door.

Candy answered with her hair a mess. It made no difference to him, but as soon as she saw who it had been, she closed the door and shouted she'd be a minute.

It was closer to five minutes before she answered it. "Cotton?"

"Candy." He giggled. "Hey, Cotton Candy. There's a strange coincidence." He held the flowers out to her. "You are right, I needed a good night's sleep to think about it. My mom used to say that sometimes love found itself in strange ways. I know from all the rumors, and what I saw the other day, you have to end up with Darren for your business. It's just that, I have my own family business."

Candy took the flowers but looked skeptically at him. "What do you mean?"

"I have no one special in my life, Candy. We can get to know each other while you try to make Darren jealous? If we feel like there is a connection, we could marry each other instead." Cotton wished he could frame that look on her face. "Divorce, if it didn't work, is possible. Second chances though, that's not. If we try this, I'll lie about a fake marriage, and I wouldn't ask anything in return."

"Nothing in return. Really? Cotton, I-I don't know what to say. Do you want to come in?"

Tempting but Cotton knew his place. "Tonight I'll come over around seven. I have to go to work right now. Just keep me in mind, and if you need to, invite Darren."

"Oh, wait." Candy reached out her hand to touch his arm. "I never got around to asking your last name."

"Tai-uh . . ." He went with a human name of Cotton Tail, but that would be too close. "Lor. Taiuhlor. It's foreign, so everyone just calls me Cotton." Close call.

"Okay. I-I'll see you tonight, Cotton."

"**B**ig Bunny, here, let me see you." Candy adjusted his the big orange bow she put on him. "Please be good. He could be a potential second chance to survival."

He was Big Bunny for six months and she never flinched an eye. He is in his human form one day and he already had her if he wanted her. He tried not to sound jealous of himself, but getting gussied up in an orange bow all for Cotton? "How do you know he's better than Darren? You don't know anything about him. He could be a serial killer."

Candy let go of the orange bow. "If he wanted to kill me he wouldn't propose a company marriage, he'd just take out Darren so I couldn't save myself. Besides, he seemed sweet, and I did go on a 'sort of' date. It's not like I have much choice, Big Bunny. It's Cotton or Darren, either way."

"I have a way out too."

"Becoming a rabbit and making magic baskets to stop the almighty apocalypse?" Candy laughed it off. "Being a bunny rabbit would really take some getting used to."

It wasn't even a possibility to her. There were actually many places underground where he could be human, but he couldn't risk taking her while she didn't know he was Cotton. "Of course, who could ever live like me?"

"Oh, I didn't mean it like that. I could," Candy said meeting her eyes to his. "I could learn if it was necessary. I just don't think I really belong down there though."

Big Bunny felt her adjust his bow again. As soon as she turned, he snuck out the back window. Being prepared, he got Cotton's clothes on and headed to her front door.

As Cotton, he knocked. He rewarded Candy with a large smile and a box of chocolates. She already thought after that date he was a little light in the head, so forgetting she couldn't have candy would be expected. She took the chocolates and invited him in. "My tastebuds can't have these yet." She set them on the counter. "I made spaghetti. I made it out of spiraled cucumbers." She moved around the counter and brought it toward him. "I hope you like it."

"I bet I will." Cotton took the plate. He'd already got into it more than once when Candy wasn't looking in his rabbit form. She ate much less than him as he gave her his madeup story of his home and family life.

She in turn told him about her mother, her relationship with her father, yadda yadda. It was nothing he had not heard as her number one confidante before. Surprisingly though, her bunny was talked about more than anything.

Was he really the *only* positive thing going on in her life? She talked about how most days all she wanted to do was come home to her pet rabbit and lie beside him. She skipped the talking since she wouldn't tell a stranger about that. Let Cotton into her life and maybe marriage? That was fine, but let him know her bunny could talk? That was a no-no.

She respected Big Bunny more than she respected herself.

As they spoke, Cotton began to rethink things. Maybe . . .

Was Candy's ancestral blood still running through her thick enough that she could love him, even as Big Bunny? "You talk a lot about that bunny of yours."

"I don't have much else going for me right now," Candy insisted. "I just . . ." She shrugged.

"Normal people don't like their pets *that* much." Cotton had to test himself. "If you come to live with me, would this bunny follow along?"

One phrase. Just that one simple phrase was all it really took to see the truth. In his other form, he didn't see it. She used the word pet. She called him a pet name. He got a collar. But here she was, with someone she believed could take her away from the bad world coming, and . . .

"My bunny is part of me."

Cotton pushed harder. "It's a pet. I can stand a cat, or maybe a dog. Bunnies are kind of pushing it though, don't you think?"

"No, I don't. Are you allergic to them?"

"No."

"Then if you marry me, it's settled."

Cotton tried hard, really hard not to smile as he clinked glasses with her. He understood it now. "Okay. For you, you could bring him. Where is he though?"

"He didn't seem fond of getting to meet you. He's quite protective of me."

"He's a freaking bunny."

"Doesn't matter." She moved away a moment to find him, but Cotton already knew it was a lost cause. Not wanting her to believe that Big Bunny left, he pretended that he saw something with an orange bow pass by him.

The rest of the night, Candy stirred conversations more toward Cotton. He changed the names of a lot of things, but told her some things about his real self. His dad dying when he was younger. How it made the family business even harder. He told her about his friend

Matt and how they met. He even told her why they went to Sweet Meats in the first place.

That caused a strange reaction. "Poured has been madly in love with Stephen since she was fourteen. They are engaged to be married. There is no way she'd flirt with anyone, ever."

Huh. That was strange. Then why did Matt think he had a chance? Cotton placed it in the back of his mind for now. Before he left, he shook Candy's hand and said goodbye.

After he left, Candy headed to the fridge. Now that Cotton was taken care of, she needed to focus on the next thing. She took out some eggs and set them aside as she boiled water. She had just placed the eggs into the boiling water as she saw familiar paws come around the corner. "There you are. You didn't come out to see Cotton at all."

"He looked like a jerk."

Her bunny would say that. Candy smiled, strolled over to him and picked him up. "Eggs?"

"You hate me."

"How about a special spaghetti made with carrots?"

"You love me."

Candy sat him next to the counter to a second dish she had been preparing in secret. Even better than the computer, a spaghetti dish made with finely cut strips of carrots. His absolute favorite. She watched him almost shove his nose into it as she got him a plate and dished it up. "Here you go." She moved back toward the eggs and took them out one at a time. With Big Bunny consumed with his meal, she set to work getting out some tools she brought from Sweet Meats.

It hit her today while she was working how she could make those little gift baskets stand out. She wasn't surprised when Big Bunny asked what she was doing. "It's called killing two birds with one stone. The eggs take up so much room because they stay fresh. You have thousands of them down there. Meanwhile, I decorate a special egg for every table that comes to Sweet Meats. It's sort of our way to say thanks for stopping by." She took a brush, dipped it in pink ink and set the egg in an egg stand. Carefully she started to draw lines across it. "It's unique decoration. Multitudes of these in a basket, and you have something special."

"Boiled eggs?" Big Bunny didn't sound half as enthused as he sucked up his carrot spaghetti.

"The older eggs I would assume are the furthest away from the hens. They'll never hatch. They are perfect." She watched his eyes of uncertainty again. "You need to trust me. Candy is a good start, but kids need something special too. Boiled eggs are tough, but oh so yummy."

"Candy and decorated boiled eggs." He tried to hide his groan, but Candy heard it regardless. "Even boiled, they'll bump all around. You'll need some kind of stuffing."

"A good point. Nothing too heavy though." Candy looked around herself. "Cotton?"

"What about him?"

"No, I mean cotton as a filling." Candy headed to her room where she had a little fake basket. She dumped it. It mostly had some sewing needles and minor things she could easily replace. She brought it out and looked around. "I don't know if I have cotton."

Big Bunny munched happily on his large plate of carrot spaghetti, but placed his paws on it. "Here you go." He pushed down on it. "Even better. Everyone should get carrot spaghetti or cucumber spaghetti. Great if the kid doesn't like sweets, they can eat the grass. Er, spaghetti."

Okay, okay. Candy gave into the request. It was soft and the candy and eggs would be supported without moving around so much. "We have to make sure the inside is lined in each basket."

"Great! Because this shredded carrot is something we can make easily on our conveyor belt." Big Bunny hopped over toward her, standing on his haunches and nestling her chin. "Candy, you've been amazing. Will you come back tonight again with me?"

"Yes, but there is still something missing." Candy looked at the basket. The eggs were great. The candy worked. The only thing missing was something saying who it was from. "Talking bunnies have to be the most magical thing I've ever seen, and I'm no child." Candy touched the basket. "You should let them know that. Kids know magic, but intellectual bunnies? What did you say they used to call your great ancestor?"

"Many different things. One of them that stuck the most was Easter Bunny."

"Then the Easter Bunny. Big Bunny, that should be your brand. The talking bunny who hops around delivering baskets to good boys and girls." Candy smiled, it was coming together better now.

Big Bunny tilted his head, making his ear flop over his left eye. "How do I do that? Leave a note?"

"No, leave a calling card. Leave a mystery inside the basket somehow."

"Hmm. Hey, last time we were at the store, they had chocolate animals." Big Bunny hopped up and down. "The biggest piece of candy, make it similar. Maybe chicks too if we can find any."

"And wolves?" Candy said it just to rile him up. He acted like he wanted to represent everything, but she doubted wolves would be in the package. "Bunnies and chicks. Let's go stock up."

Big Bunny headed toward his usual basket. He couldn't normally go into a store, but Candy had always taken him anyhow in a giant picnic basket with a cover that opened on both sides. Come to think of it? Candy looked around her apartment. She had all kinds of things for Big Bunny. "Big Bunny?"

Big Bunny shoved his nose out of the basket. It twitched. "Yep?"

Candy picked up the basket. "Do you think I am obsessed with you?" He stuck his head most of the way out of the basket. "I've got bedding near every window. I sleep by your side each night. I don't give you regular food, I prepare every meal you eat." She fidgeted her fingers. "Cotton thought I was obsessed. Am I crazy?"

"See? You are already having problems. Ditch him and come with me." Big Bunny winked at her and hid himself back in his basket. "Store. Grab as many as you can and let's head back to the hole. I'll give you the directions this time."

"Good because you kidnapping me in a truck didn't sit well," Candy said as she headed out the door.

She cared for her bunny. She wasn't obsessed with him. She wasn't. Right?

CUTE BASKETS DON'T BITE

Candy was so tempted to buy every animal. They even had a giraffe in their chocolate collection. She packed all the rabbits in on the other side of the picnic basket, along with some chicks. She saw the wolves, but knew better. There was something about wolves that Big Bunny truly hated.

"Candy."

Oh no. Darren Manner walked over toward her. She hid the last piece of chocolate away. "Darren."

"Your mom told me you kissed a Vegan." Darren wrapped his arm around her. Candy heard a low growl from her basket. She patted the top to make him hush up. "So?"

"Yes, Posh pushed me. You saw it." Candy pushed him aside. "Remember, your new fiancé?"

"Oh, that. Well, I don't know. A ring is a ring." Darren followed her to the register. "I kind of want to see what your mom was talking about, and I think I might be?" He gestured to the basket. "Is the adorable bunny in there?"

"Uh?" She blushed. "Yes, but don't tell."

Darren covered his mouth in delight with a chuckle. "Can I see it? I'll be careful." He lifted the lid. "Oh, it's twitching it's nose." He quickly lowered it. "Candy Sweet, you're so sweet you took a bunny illegally into a store."

"Let's not say that out so loud," she reminded him.

"I love bunnies. So, this other guy though? Rumor is you want to marry the guy you kissed?"

Boy, that rumor spread ultra fast! That was good luck for her, they could discuss it naturally now. "His family has a company too. Since I lose everything as it stands, if you end up with Posh, then I'm thinking about marrying him."

"Are you really going to be with a Vegan?" Darren chuckled at her. "You know? I know you can't taste sweet right now. I can overcome that. I am Spice."

Once again, Candy patted her growling basket. "Cotton has treated me fine. He's even the one who offered to marry me if we hit it off."

"What?" Darren's smile wiped clean off his face. "Your momma didn't tell me that, I thought it was your idea?"

"Momma doesn't know everything." Candy took the pieces of chocolate out of the basket and set them on the counter. "He is much sweeter than you."

Darren grabbed his chest like she stabbed his heart. "Ouch. But hey, I bet he can't give you the riches I can. I doubt his company is anything nearly as much as what we could have. I was willing to settle for forty percent. You would be going for ten percent of Sweet Meats to over sixty percent."

"I share with my mom and my sister, it's twenty percent each."

"Still better than what he could give you." Darren laid his hand way too close to the basket. He brought it up right away. "Ow!"

"Silly, Darren." Candy picked up her groceries and stuffed them in the basket. "Cute baskets don't bite." She walked off before anyone else said a word.

"This was better." Candy adjusted her rabbit ear as she made her way back down Bunny Hill's hole. "See? You should have asked me last time instead of kidnapping me."

"I was afraid you might reject me if you saw me as—"

Candy watched Big Bunny but he stopped. "What? Transform into a human? It shouldn't be that big of a surprise, I suppose."

"I didn't say human. Just, something."

Candy had expected to head down and see the same veggie conveyor belts working, but the other rabbits were nowhere to be seen. As she got closer through the holes, she could see why.

Somehow, they had duplicated her candy. Hundreds of baskets were being lined with special candies held by each bunny down one conveyor belt. "The hens?" She guessed.

"No, everyone has different powers. That is the result of my mother's main power," Big Bunny answered. "That is why we bought all the bars. She can duplicate each to their full extent."

Along the wall there were already hundreds more baskets. "How many children are in the city?"

"We don't do just the city." Big Bunny winked at her as he touched her floppy ear. "We do the world."

The world? The world?! "How?" She gestured toward the twenty rabbits around them. "You need a much bigger workforce."

"That isn't all the bunnies here," Big Bunny said. "Not even one percent. Rabbits multiply like . . .well, rabbits. You haven't even touched a full one percent of our little society here."

Wow. Candy looked behind him as his mother came back around. He talked with her a little, and then his mother wrapped her arms around Candy.

"Carrot grass good, Candy of legend!"

Of course, he must have mentioned the carrot and cucumber sliced spaghetti. Carrot grass, good name for it. Candy felt her head being patted by his mother before she finally let go.

All night long, Candy helped boil eggs, and brushes were actually found for her size (okay, a little larger) to decorate them. Lying them in along with the baskets, others picked up on what she had done too. The cucumber and carrot shredding was easy to mimic with their old conveyor belts.

"Great job." Big Bunny hopped over by her. "I'm proud of you, Candy."

Candy tried to hide the strange blush. Her fur was white but she was afraid she might be turning red. For some reason, Big Bunny made her feel funnier the longer she was around him in that form. Bunny rabbit to bunny rabbit, it must have been something to do with that. Surely she didn't really see him as anything more than her sweet pet. Surely. "I would have been a hen." She looked toward Big Bunny. "If I had been a creature, right?"

"Maybe. Maybe a duck. Who knows?" Big Bunny moved closer to her. She felt his warm, soft furry lip tickle against her floppy ear. "Although, I think you make a fine bunny rabbit."

A fine rabbit. She doubted rabbits should be getting that warm beneath their fur or it'd catch on fire.

"Are you okay, Candy?"

"Fine." How warped was she? Cotton was right. She was obsessed with her rabbit. She might even be . . . "I-I really need to get out of here soon."

"Sure, we can go home if you are ready."

We. Yes. When she was human and he was just the cute little rabbit, she was much better off.

"Good morning, Cotton." Candy welcomed him into Sweet Meats to his usual table. They'd been seeing each other for more than two weeks now, every night and every day at Sweet Meats. She didn't really give into the whole 'make Darren jealous' thing. There just didn't seem to a reason to, except to taste sweet again. That just wasn't worth it to her.

"Back again?" Poured came over to the table too with a snicker. "Can't you just go on a date instead of stalk my sister at work?"

Honestly. Cotton was a thousand times better than Darren. They even did the traditional dinner and a movie. He was always a gentleman. "The usual?"

"It's about all I can afford," Cotton teased. "Yep, five, twenty nine."

"The most expensive way to buy water," Poured said as she left the table. Cotton and Candy both ignored her. Neither Momma Sweet, Darren or Poured were going to stop him being a customer.

"Do you think your sister will ever like me?" Cotton asked before Candy left with the order. Candy simply shrugged. She knew if she picked Cotton, Poured and Momma would be looking at tougher times as well. It didn't make them very fond of him.

Candy headed toward the back to get the water. Tonight she'd make up for it when he came over for a date. It was understandable that Momma and Poured were angry over Cotton, but she couldn't figure out her Big Bunny's actions.

From day one he hid from Cotton. He never stayed in the same room. For six months, Candy had raised Big Bunny alone, and she thought maybe he was scared Cotton would ruin everything. Maybe he thought Candy wouldn't be able to show him the same amount of attention?

Or, maybe, Big Bunny being next to her as a real bunny was confusing him too. As much as she liked Cotton, she couldn't stop thinking about Big Bunny's idea too. There should be no way that she'd rather sit in a hole, work on a conveyor belt and make baskets every day. Yet, every time Big Bunny took her down that rabbit hole, he showed her more. He showed her deeper parts. He even showed her one of the 'city' dwellings where bunny rabbits just like him had socialized and lived at.

Candy would bet about everything she owned that she'd already seen more than there was room on Big Bunny hill. The holes kept extending downward and upward into different hills.

She also learned how they protected themselves. When everyone knew Big Bunny was coming, it was easy to come through the holes. There were actual guards with massive steel doors. Each hole inside the dwelling was guarded heavily so no chance hunter might try to stick poison or smoke down there to make anyone come out.

Although he shared so much though, he still held secrets. So many secrets. He refused to tell her his real name. He refused to tell her if he transformed to a human or what he looked like in his other form. Not even his hair color. He vowed it was to keep their relationship simple because knowing anything else would make it too awkward to keep him as a pet.

Somehow, she was beginning to doubt that same old excuse.

Realizing she was thinking about her bunny instead of serving Cotton again, she shook her head. She had to stop being ridiculous. Before she reached his table though, Cotton was standing next to it, side by side with Darren.

"This whole charade is getting annoying," Darren said as he poked Cotton in the chest. "Just step aside so I can marry Candy. I gave up on Posh, I want her."

Candy came out and broke the two of them up. "Cotton, your drink." She sat it down but looked over at Darren. "You have no business here."

"I do!" Darren gestured to Cotton. "Are you going to marry him or not?"

Candy wanted to slug him right then and there. She had time left.

"Candy, is it me you want?" Cotton met her eye to eye. "I don't want you to settle. Tell me there is no one else you'd want."

Candy turned from his eye as she saw the vision of her bunny again. Gaw, what was wrong with her?! Cotton was the greatest. She did like him, it was just . . .*something*. Something was wrong about him.

"Candy doesn't completely." Poured saw the opportunity. "She can't look you in the eye. She must like Darren more than she lets on."

Oh no way, that wasn't even funny. Candy glared at Poured. She would ruin everything.

"Candy?" Cotton questioned her again. "Look me in the eyes, and tell me you'd be happy with me?"

"I would." She said it, but not to his eyes. She tried again, but her voice faltered. "I-I would."

"No, Candy." Cotton stood up. "You're a nice girl. Sweetest one ever, but your heart has to be completely mine."

No. No, no, no! "It is though, I do care."

Cotton looked toward Poured and then at Candy. "Five days from now, I'll come by your apartment, Candy. I may not have your heart, but I won't leave you to Darren alone. I'll give you a chance with my company. Just, not as my wife. You have more skills we can explore for it."

Cotton. Candy wanted to go after him, but she didn't know what to say. Her voice failed her. Her eyes failed her. She liked Cotton, and she would have chosen him any day for marriage over Darren.

In five days, Cotton would offer some small deal with his company to avoid having to marry Darren. The thought pushed too hard now. Not this, not after all that time of getting to know him. She thought they had a great chance together. Why couldn't she say she'd be happy with him? *Why?* She ran out the door with only one goal in mind.

Candy sniffled as she rushed into her home. She closed the door, seeking the furry companion she always had before. "Big Bunny."

Her body slid down the door, unable to even want to get up to look for him. He had always come to her front door.

She wasn't mistaken as he hopped over to her. He moved into her lap and she touched his big floppy ears. They always made her feel a little better, but even that wouldn't work today.

"Candy, what is it?" he asked as he stood on his haunches and twitched his nose at her.

"Cotton. I let him go." Candy could barely open her eyes. "He was there for me. He was offering marriage. He was polite, funny . . .but something happened. I couldn't say he was the one who made me happy."

"Oh no." Big Bunny hugged her tighter. "Now what?"

"Five days. He'll offer me something at his company. If it's not enough though, then I'm off to marry Darren." Candy gulped. "I think Sweet Meats is just an undeniable road I have to follow."

"No, you don't have too." Big Bunny thumped his foot on her lightly. "Stay with me at Bunny Hill."

It may have seemed at first that such a request was laughable. Living underground with bunny rabbits and chickens? More than once she had considered it, but every time something inside said it wouldn't be right. She wasn't a real bunny, she was a fake bunny. The white fur with blonde streaks, the floppy ears, the light hopping around the ground. She wished with all her heart that it felt right, but it didn't.

Big Bunny was still just Big Bunny. He wasn't a human. Maybe he turned human, but he never once confirmed it, and her relationship was becoming unhealthy with the rabbit. Her human self was getting further away each day.

She closed her eyes, sitting up and feeling Big Bunny slide off her lap. That was it. That was the biggest problem. It was why she couldn't give her heart to anyone else. It was a fact that she didn't want to face. No one did such a thing. It was wrong, flat out wrong. Talking rabbit or not, she was sick in the head. Absolutely sick, but she knew the undeniable truth.

She couldn't completely love Cotton because somehow she had also loved her bunny.

"Candy?"

"Sweet Meats is my future." Candy sniffled again and got up off the floor. "Sweet Meats is my future." She heard him hopping along beside her to her bedroom but she closed the door on him. He rubbed his paw against it, but she couldn't let him in. He couldn't be at the foot of her bed anymore. He couldn't be curled up near her anymore.

"Come to Bunny Hill with me."

"I am not a bunny rabbit!" She yelled at him as she grabbed a pillow and threw it at the closed door. She didn't hear his voice again after that. She stayed in her room for some time, trying to figure out when it happened. Why it happened.

When she changed into a rabbit? Sooner? Later? She had been obsessed with that bunny rabbit ever since she saved him. Was it an unhealthy obsession that turned into love, or did it happen when he started changing her into his form?

When it got later, she opened the door. Unable to resolve her feelings, she could not let him starve. "Big Bunny, I'm sorry." She called for him as she started to cut up some fresh carrots, but he never answered.

When she went looking for him, all she found was an open window.

FROM FRUIT BASKET TO CANDY BASKET

"Cotton?" Lop-eared Matt said as he hopped over to him. "The product is almost in place. We'll need to start getting magic distribution users on our first shipment. I just need your permission, Cotton."

Cotton stared at the basket in front of him. It was a random basket out of thousands around them. A simple brown basket made a little extra special with a bow set in the middle. On the top were a few pieces of candy and four decorated boiled eggs. Below that was more candy that fell into the carrot spaghetti grass cushioning it. On the side, the large chocolate bunny had been duplicated as well as several smaller versions of chicks.

It wasn't a fruit basket, it was a Candy basket. He took his paw and wiped at his face. "Ever love a bunny rabbit that wasn't really a bunny rabbit, Matt?"

"Just that crush at Sweet Meats. Although, I don't get it. I'm not thick, Cotton, she had flirted with me." Matt hopped away missing the entire real point of the conversation.

"Yeah. I mean, these descendants, they are just too far removed." He touched the bow at the top of the basket. A shiny orange and pink that changed according to the direction of the light.

He had everything. Cotton had everything, and he let it slip away because of the wolf. He needed to tell Candy who he had been, but he wanted more reassurance. That fault was supposed to turn her away and toward Big Bunny, but it didn't work out the way he had pictured it.

What doe rabbit really wanted to come live underground with a buck like him? He saw realization pass in her eyes and it freaked her out. She wasn't ready yet.

Nor would she be. Cotton promised on day five he'd come to her with some kind of deal. If he didn't, Darren would get his wolfish hands on her sooner, and she'd lose Sweet Meats.

"Cotton, the storm is getting extra heavy," Matt said as he came over again. "The first fleet of Easter Bunnies can't even get out. What should we do?"

Stalled before they even started. It didn't matter though, it was the fifth day, and he had to get back to Candy.

"That weather is flat out crazy," Poured said as she strolled over to Candy. "Don't worry, I'm sure he'll still come."

Candy barely looked at her. Ever since that day with Cotton, Poured and Momma became more reasonable again. Saying they were sorry that it didn't work out.

"Momma said tonight should be the night," Poured said as she handed Candy a glass of water. "Poppa Sweet isn't looking so well."

Candy wouldn't know. She hadn't seen 'Poppa' Marlen in so long. She never even really saw him sick. . .no, her imagination was getting away from her. Her father and her were like strangers, and she hadn't actually tried to see him when he was sick. Losing father would be devastating toward the business, so why would Momma be making something like that up? It was just an eerie feeling. Poured and Momma smiled too much in her direction. "Poured?"

"Yes, Candy?" Poured said as she came back over.

"I want to see Poppa Sweet." Candy watched Poured's eyes.

"Why? You never cared to before. He doesn't do much." Poured didn't meet her eyes to her again. "You're just worried about Cotton. Don't worry, I'm sure he'll show and offer some kind of job."

Candy wasn't half as nervous though as Poured was about him showing up. She could see it. Sweet Meats was holding something back. Everything in her life, someone was always hiding something. Couldn't anyone be straight with her, just once?

"Psst."

Candy looked at her feet and almost flipped. What was he doing there? "This is a highly dangerous area." She picked up Big Bunny and set him on the table. She meticulously checked his paws, worry overcoming her. She hadn't seen him in five days.

"Today is the big day. A little rough start, but come. It's your vision, you should be a part of it," Big Bunny said.

"I have to wait for Cotton."

"We'll go visit him if necessary. Please, Candy?"

Those big, sad bunny rabbit eyes. Even now, she just couldn't say no to them. Not after being gone for so long.

Just one more time as a bunny rabbit, that was it. Just for him. Then, no more bunny rabbit life. She could keep the real life in focus. Sweet Meats.

Just one more time.

She drove the truck he always seemed to have. She'd watched him drive it one time completely with magic. Steering wheel and gas pedal ran on their own. The windows were quite tinted though so no one could see it was a bunny rabbit driving.

Did he always drive it with magic? Did he become human and drive it? How did he manage to get it? A guessing game, that's all it ever had been. As she drove though, she saw her phone ringing. Big Bunny took over with his magic on the driving as she answered. "Hello?"

"Candy, damn it! Where are you? Are you with Cotton? No one saw him come in."

"No."

"Then get back here! What if you miss him? Do you have any idea how bad that would be?"

Candy lifted her ear away from the phone's shouting. "Something came up."

"They sure are obsessed over that guy." Big Bunny moved closer to the phone, eyeing it suspiciously. "We haven't even been gone five minutes."

"He'll be back." Candy touched her forehead. "I am hanging up now, Poured, I will be back later. It's not the end of the world if I miss Cotton."

"Yes it is!"

Candy groaned and hung up, but Big Bunny shook his head. "What?"

"That 'yes it is' was strange."

"It is to her. She wants the twenty percent of Sweet Meats, so . . .?" Hm. Why was she worried about Cotton then? She should probably be happy if Candy missed him and had to marry Darren. "That doesn't make any sense."

"I just can't shake the feeling it's more with Poured." Big Bunny wiggled his paws extra hard at the wheel. "If I form a bubble around the truck, would people see it in this blizzard?"

"Oh just let me drive."

Candy hopped her familiar hop toward the hole on Bunny Hill. She'd done this several times, but it felt bittersweet knowing this would be the last time. She moved down the darkness without fear and came out toward the light.

The doe and buck rabbits were all smiling right beside the hen and roosters. In the corners, baby bunnies and chicks were playing with each other. The baskets were filled and it was a sight beyond compare. These were no ordinary baskets someone would mistake as fruit.

They were dreamy. The colors. The unique combination of elements, and topped off professionally with a chocolate bunny. Kids would go ga ga for these magic baskets the Easter Bunnies would be bringing. "Easter Bunny baskets." She was happy that she decided to come back. All of the work transforming this place, she had to come see it.

Big Bunny would be safe no matter what life threw at her now. Not only that, her life felt like it had a purpose these last two weeks. Sure, some of her ideas could never get through, but the ones that she believed in the most did. "Throughout the world."

Oh, Bunny Hill was definitely bigger.

WHY HIDE EGGS?

Hop by hop, she was doing the last part to help her bunny. Although small, each bunny had a set of houses they would hit that morning. Too small to hold the real baskets, they had strange magical packets that would be placed in an open area. When no eye was looking at them, they were supposed to change into baskets.

Candy had to admit that magic before really didn't have much appeal anymore. But the rabbits, those Easter Bunny rabbits, they had real magic. Duplication, multiplication, transformation, transportation, etc. The list went on and many had more than one power. The children, when they saw these baskets, they were going to be mystified.

The trip to their first home was not easy. Magic did not completely work like clockwork. Unless they were in a bind, they were expected to get into the house themselves. Only when it could not be contained were they supposed to hit another packet standing right next to the house. It would take them five feet to the left. Although inside the house, Candy's first try almost had her falling off of a chair.

There was something else strange about the baskets. Before she left, half the time, some of the eggs went missing. She knew how many had been in the baskets, so it was no surprise when she finally saw magic working against her.

Big Bunny tried to hide it, but it was no use. She moved over to a vase in the room, and searched around for the egg. Feeling it with her paw, she left it there, but shook her head. "Why are you hiding the eggs?"

"Because no kid needs a dozen eggs to eat."

"We have been through this. They won't eat all the eggs at once, and most will share with their family."

"Yes, but, candy is already right there." Big Bunny gestured to the basket. "That is your magic candy, that is fine, but twelve eggs? Eggs are eggs. No one should eat twelve eggs at once." He gestured around himself. "Instructions were given to hide at least half of them."

"From who?"

"My mother." He didn't say it with a ton of pride, and a bit of shame. However he was following her instructions, so Candy had to admit defeat. At least the children could get up and go look for the eggs. They were clearly easy to spot, and no kid would miss them for long.

"**I**t would not be full time."

Candy looked back at Big Bunny as he spoke. They were on their last house. So far, the day had been fun. She didn't return back to Sweet Meats yet, choosing to play the part of Easter Bunny with her bunny. However, she knew it would be coming to an end soon.

"It would not be full time," Big Bunny said yet again as he hopped over to her. "Stay."

"What do you mean full time?"

"You do not have to be a rabbit full time," he said. "There is room down in the holes for bigger creatures. You could change back and forth."

No, she could not. Candy closed her eyes. "I would be a human rabbit."

"There is nothing wrong with that."

"How could you know?" Candy hopped away. "Life would just get twisted. Can I run Sweet Meats or do I let Momma take charge while I hop around?"

"You are happier here," Big Bunny stated. "You are happier with me than you would ever be at Sweet Meats."

"You hate wolves!" Candy turned around and yelled.

"What does that have to do with anything?"

"It is their way of life," Candy said, "and I do not see you rebelling against nature." She hopped a little closer. "Why do you hate them that much?"

"Because they are vicious killers. The wolf gene is still out there, but the pure wolves are not. That wolf gene, that makes hunters. People who want to kill us. They are wolves. With their shotguns and ammo, they are just modern day renditions. We still die to them. My father died to them." Big Bunny went silent. "They take everything away."

"Then I cannot stay."

"Why?"

"Because I am giving myself to a wolf."

"What?"

Candy tried to his smile, but it was hopeless. "Darren Manner."

"You cannot go to Darren Manner." His emerald green eyes turned red again. "You are waiting for Cotton."

"For what? To hurt him even more?" Candy began to hop away. "I am tired of hurting the ones I love. Momma. Poured. Cotton. For my own selfish need. Seeing him again, it would just hurt both of us." She stopped. "Change me back, I need to get going."

"No."

"You cannot stop this." Candy's voice broke. "I didn't help you for the apocalypse, I helped you find a better home. I will not make you live with the wolf. Now, change me back."

Candy waited at the first table at Sweet Meats. Poured came over again as she had done before.

"I am glad you're back. You don't want to miss your Cotton," she said. "Do you want something to eat?"

"It's Darren." Candy turned to look toward Poured. "I can't deny facts, it's the way it has always been. Darren will be coming. We'll elope first, I talked him into it for a fifty fifty cut. Then, we'll go from there." Poured should have been thrilled by the news. Instead, she dropped her tray.

"You can't do that!" Poured touched her shoulder. "You have to be with Cotton."

"I am saving Sweet Meats, not just myself with some charitable part time job." What else did Poured want from her? "Watch out for Posh trying to interrupt his way over, please. I want to get this done as soon as possible."

"But you can't!"

"Why not?" Candy groaned as she glared at her sister. "You hated Cotton, what difference does it make?"

"An apocalyptic difference." Momma Sweet came to Candy's other side. "Candy, you don't get a choice. You have to be with Cotton."

"Apocalyptic?" Candy looked from Poured to Momma. Why would they use that term? Her mother and sister sat down and shared it. They shared everything. The dream when she was five. Tricking Cotton and Posh to come in at the right time.

"Poppa Sweet isn't even ill, I told him to take six months off at a beach resort somewhere while I spread rumors. He knows the dream too," her mother revealed. "You need to feel a mutual love for this Cotton. Then, when everything gets better, you can marry Darren."

"You." Candy sat there, frozen. This whole time. Her family had been scheming against her. "Your translation isn't even right," she said as she sat up from the chair. Then, Cotton came in. Poured and

Momma tried to rush her over toward the door, but she didn't move. He would just have to come to her.

"Candy." Cotton bowed politely toward her. "We have some unfinished business."

"No, we don't." Candy gestured to her mother and sister at her sides. "It was all an elaborate setup by them. I refuse to fall for anything more. I am getting married to Darren and that's final. Leave."

"Candy," Cotton tried again. "We need to talk."

"Leave."

"You have to be with *him*!" Her mother whispered sharply in her ear. It was loud enough though that Cotton heard it. Candy didn't care. "Fall in love with him already, Candy!"

"The apocalypse is not about me and Cotton falling in love, it was about helping bunnies save the world by entertaining children!" Candy yelled at the both of them. Candy looked toward Cotton, and then back at her family. "It's because of you two that I can't be where I really *want* to be!" Candy left out the door. There was nothing more anyone could say to her.

Cotton strolled over to Momma and Poured Sweet with purpose. "What prophecy? What have you been doing?"

"Everyone knows it. You should know it too, it's just that no one knew who it would be for. Or, exactly what it means sometimes." Momma Sweet sighed. "It's been around since civilization began."

"Every prophecy isn't how it sounds," Cotton argued. "Tell me it. Pretend I'm an idiot."

"I think Candy is the idiot," Poured interrupted. "Even she knows it. There's nothing about bunnies or anything. Nothing except the name. How did she come up with helping bunnies?"

"Prophecy, *now*." Cotton didn't have time to waste.

"Sweet Candy, Candy Sweet. Delicious power with Vegan treat."

Candy's name was in it, but Cotton didn't hear anything else in it.

"That's just part one of the currently accepted translation. Its rhyming in parts, mostly its just mish mashed words. It's complicated, and the translations are what most people go by in the back. Whoever came up with it was mad." Poured moved over towards the counter and brought a large book over to Cotton. "Here you go."

"This whole book?"

"Yep."

That wasn't a prophecy, it was a book. It was decorated with a religious flair and inscriptions on the sides. He opened it and flipped through the middle.

"Candy coated chocolate bunnies. Egg. Ending. Hole. Bunny Hill. Queen. Not mad. Mirror. Fall. All fall. Fire. Winter. Egg. Chocolate. Candy. Wonder. Rabbit. Hatter. Red. Hearts." Cotton handed the book back. "Who wrote it?"

"No one knows. It's the oldest piece of literature we have." Poured placed it back behind the counter. "It's like that through most of the book, but there are some sections that make sense."

"There is a part of the book that predicts that a woman named Candy Sweet must be with a man named Cotton Tail," Momma Sweet answered. "It could have been anyone, but at five years old my little girl had a vivid dream no child ever should. She had never even known about the book of prophecy at that age."

"Spring is Winter, Winter is Spring. Time was getting closer," Poured said softly. "It's all over if she marries the wolf."

Cotton shook his head and headed out the door. The book was definitely by someone who had written their own prophecies, but they were focusing on different sections. Whether it was Candy's world's prophecy, or the bunny's prophecy didn't matter.

He just knew he couldn't lose Candy.

Even though it was cold outside, children were hanging by windows and by their doors, showing off their baskets.

"This is crazy," she heard one mother note. "It's a candy-filled basket. All the kids have them." Candy noticed the mother glance at her. "How?"

"It's all over the TV," another one commented "Worldwide! Baskets filled with candy and eggs hiding around the house."

Candy couldn't help a small smirk. Egg hiding, how ridiculous, but everyone followed Cotton's mother. Eh, might as well call him by his real name. When her family said they were going by prophecy, she knew it was Cotton *Tail*. Odd name, unless you were a rabbit. She never saw him transform, but there were bigger areas in Bunny Hill that they could pass through. Something humans could move through. The fact that Big Bunny never came out when Cotton came around. A part of her, maybe an inkling, always had suspicions, but when her family revealed they did it for the prophecy, that was it.

Cotton Tail was Big Bunny. He tried so hard to save her from the wolf, but that rabbit didn't understand. She watched another kid come running out of the house, miraculously not falling on the ice.

The concept had been brilliant. People still didn't know who sent it, but everyone did comment on the large chocolate bunnies. It might take some time for the branding to seep through, but people would soon associate those Easter Bunny baskets to Easter Bunnies. All those magical rabbits. For a short time, she even got to be one.

She dismissed the thought though and watched as Darren came toward her. Momma and Poured Sweet were wrong, the rabbits had the real prophecy. Candy's world had never made sense, just loose translations. The rabbits though, they had more concrete pieces. Maybe the whole thing used to be one long ago when everyone had been the same? She didn't know, nor did she care. Candy stopped as Darren came up to her, giving her a kiss on the cheek. "Darren."

"I was on my way over." He rubbed his hands together while his breath hung in the air. "You got the fifty fifty contract? Because Posh was willing sixy forty. You are naturally cute, but I've got to make sure. My family begins cutting me off next year."

"Suing for currency rights may have been a bit showy I suppose?" He didn't answer back. "Fifty fifty," Candy agreed. "Walk with me, it's only a few more blocks."

"Are you sure you don't want an extravagantly cute ceremony?" Darren asked. "We could have your cute bunny hop up with the rings tied around it. It would be darling."

"No need to, that's just wasting money and time to be goofy." Candy shrugged. They both walked side by side. The snow was coming down harder, but it made no difference to her. Her mind was set.

She put the ball in Cotton's court, whether he knew it or not.

Cotton moved as fast as he could heading down the blocks to the court. If Candy was going to marry Darren she wouldn't bother having a big ceremony. Signed papers, that was all it took. The weather didn't make it any easier. The snow had become a blizzard again and the sidewalks were getting buried. He kept his eyes open though, knowing she would head to the closest place.

Candy's family made her mad, and when they did that, she tended to become reckless. Seeing how having a successful magic basket day didn't do a thing for the weather, Candy's recklessness may result in the ending. It wouldn't be the first ending Cotton had seen, but he'd never lost anything precious in them. Not since he was young and went on his first dimension skip.

Holes. Holes in the ground, spread out all around found the dimension holes faster. If the weather didn't fix itself, his kind would be heading out again. Candy would be left behind. "Candy!"

There in the distance hiding by a building with Darren was Candy. Cotton hurried even faster, knowing the weather would prevent her from doing anything else. "Candy, I said we need to talk and I meant it!" Cotton raced with everything he had. In this form, he couldn't run half as fast, but he had to make it to her. "Candy." Now bent over, catching his breath and staring at her feet, he was nearly at the finish line. "I'm sorry about what happened. We can give it another chance."

He looked up toward her, but she didn't have love shining back in her eyes.

"You need to stop this. You made your choice," Candy answered. "I made my choice. There is no going back."

"There is always time to go back."

"Not now."

"Nothing can make me believe that."

"I've already been caught by the wolf."

That phrase made him stop. Was he too late, did they make it to the courts? "Did you get married?"

"I got caught." Candy shook her head. "You only assumed you were saving me if I waited five days from having Darren in control. Silly Rabbit. Your the one who waited and messed it up."

He looked back at her again. She knew. Somehow, she had put it together. "I'm sorry for lying. I just—"

"—it doesn't matter. At least you know the truth. At least I know the truth." Candy looked away. "Why my heart was so confused between two people that weren't even people."

"When?"

"When I found out about what Momma and Poured were up to. I had some funky suspicions but nothing I would let myself believe. Oh, but Cotton Taiuhlor for the legendary name Cotton Tail in the prophecy? Difficult last name alright." Candy placed her hand over Darren's mouth as he complained senselessly about wanting to know what was going on. "Funny thing is, if you just would have told me, we could have saved so much time." Her eyes met his confidently. "I already knew you couldn't stand wolves as a bunny, but as Cotton, you couldn't even accept a glass of water that he touched."

He should go crawl back to his hole. Darren had already won.

"Just tell me," Candy said. "Did you believe the same things? Was the goal just to get me to trust in you, to let you save me from the big, bad wolf so the world would be saved?"

"No." Cotton walked up closer to her. "No. My family didn't even plan on me getting caught in a cage. When it happened, we just went with it. I swear. It wasn't until after we met that I figured out your role, but just as the one to help save the business. I never even looked at the book of your world."

"Yeah, well." Candy shrugged. "What can you do? I hope your business is successful now because we've crossed that threshold where I have to say goodbye to you. You won't be able to stand Darren. Our relationship can never be the same."

"I know." Cotton didn't even know how to react. Darren held out his hand toward him in a friendly shake but he batted it away and glared at him. He'd never shake hands with a . . .

with a wolf? "Did it matter? That I was half and half, Candy?" He needed to know as he reached his hand out, grasping her arm gently.

She took his hand off of her arm. "Love is strange." That was the only thing she said before she turned away from the building, grabbing Darren's arm again. The snow was getting lighter again, enough to escape. Cotton stood there several seconds, thinking about what she just said. She rejected being a rabbit. She rejected Cotton. All because the wolf already had her. It was in his nature to hate wolves, but experience just deepened it.

Candy didn't reject him, she knew that he would reject her.

The only thing that had kept them apart was him. His lies and his blindness. He looked at his feet, wondering how people could ever see them as lucky. Not that they were rabbit feet right now, but he was one in the same. So was Candy. He liked her as a human or as a rabbit. She took care of him. She saved his life. She even tried to save his family's business, whether she understood the true impact of it or not.

Darren may have married her, but he still wanted her in his life. "Candy!" He rushed up toward her again. "I don't care!"

Candy turned around. "What?"

"Darren Manner." Cotton watched Posh come straight for Darren. She was waving a contract. "Seventy thirty!" Behind Posh was Momma and Poured Sweet. They snitched. Not because they cared, but because they were trying to prevent the end too.

"Seventy thirty?" Darren asked as he went toward Posh. "Who gets the seventy?"

"You, you dweeb." Posh grabbed him and kissed him on the lips. "Knock it off, let's go. I'm tired of this. You won, you get your seventy. Happy?"

It was too late for that, they were already married. He was the one who messed up. But? It shouldn't . . . keep him from ever seeing her again. Divorce was still a thing if one day she wanted to change her mind. She never would though, if he abandoned her now. "I don't care. I mean, I do, but . . .I care too much for you to let you go." He touched her cheek. "I have been a jerk not telling you everything. You haven't done anything wrong. If I found a carcass left behind that a wolf devoured, I would still have the decency to bury it." Was that the right way to put it? "I mean. I told you to stay before I knew you had been married to Darren. I still say, stay."

"As a rabbit?"

"Whatever you want. We can work from your home. Rabbit, human, I don't care." He preferred his rabbit form over his human, but for her, he'd change that. "Even. . ." Oh, to say this. "I'll try not to bite Darren."

"Would I have to stop eating meat?"

"I never stopped you before." It was still so risky. That look in her eyes. All the times he had lied to her, they were coming back into them. His past actions were being judged for and against him in her decision.

"Do you really think you deserve that? After all of the lying?" Candy looked over toward Darren and Posh. Neither of them understood a thing. She drew her attention back to Cotton. "Do you have the power to forget?"

"No." Cotton didn't know what she'd want with that power.

"Does your friend, Matt?"

"Yes."

"Good." Candy gestured the other way. "Now go home. Take your spot at the window and I will see you when I get home. If you decide not to go home, then you decide not to. It's your choice."

PINKERLINGS

In his rabbit form, Cotton waited by the window. He snuggled himself up tight in his bed, not knowing what would happen. The snow had increased again, but he didn't care anymore. Candy wanted the power of forget. She didn't say she forgave him, chose him, or despised his trickery.

It scared him more than anything. What did she want with that power? Was he supposed to forget her, or the other way around?

His thoughts were interrupted as he heard the door open. Instinctively he wanted to run and greet her. He stayed on his bed though, as she instructed.

She moved over toward him next to his bed by the window. "Did you find Matt?"

"I did."

"I want to forget that you can talk. I want my Big Bunny, before things got awkward. I don't want to remember the other rabbits, the chicks, or the hill."

Full erase. She wanted him back as her pet and nothing else. Oh, was that hard to hear! His head ducked a little further down than usual, letting his ears completely hit the ground without care. She would still be able to take care of him. He could still see her.

Just nothing else.

"Can you do it?" she asked him.

"Yeah. This time tomorrow, I could have it done." His voice was broke, but he completed the sentence. He could never be anything more than a pet to Candy, but at least he'd still have her in his life.

"You would?"

Cotton looked over toward her. "Anything to make you happy."

"Good. Then cancel that."

Cotton's ears shot up a moment before they flopped back down against him.

"You used me. You betrayed my trust and you lied to me." Candy shook her finger at him. "Naughty Big Bunny. If I didn't care so much, I would have kicked you to the curb. In adult form. I couldn't do that to you as a rabbit, you'd hurt your head."

Cotton couldn't even wrap his mind around everything he was hearing.

"Now, before I tell you anything else?" Candy gestured to him one more time. "Is there anything *else* that you have to tell me? Any more secrets that you are hiding from me? There's not some other lost part to a prophecy book out there somewhere?"

"There might have been. I believe your kind took it and began to worship it." Big Bunny chuckled, finally feeling relief.

Candy stroked his ear. She always did that when she was conflicted. "Big Bunny?"

"Cotton Tail would work better for me now," he said. Before she could say anything else he added, "I didn't know if you would love a rabbit that you only knew as a pet. I really planned on telling you." She had nothing but trust for that issue. "You'll have to trust me on that. I know I lied a lot, but from now on, I won't."

"Okay." Candy sighed. "I lied too by the way."

Cotton looked over toward her. "About what?"

"Getting married to the wolf."

"What?!" His ears shot up again before gravity brought them down along with him in her lap.

"You pushed me to the edge of sanity, buster." Candy crossed her arms, refusing to acknowledge him. "I had to push you to the edge to see if you would still want me. If you didn't, then I'd have my answer and be married to Darren with Sweet Meats making me tons of money right now." She uncrossed her arms and groaned. "Instead, Posh and Darren tied it. Momma and Poured are angry as hell I let that happen, but I'm angry at them, so . . ." She shrugged. "Life's just as messed up as ever."

No more Darren Manner. *Yes.*

"As for you, *rabbit*, I don't know what to do yet with you." Candy lifted his ear and watched it droop. "Should I help out with the next year as a rabbit, or should I help out as the human I like to be? Especially since my father is just fine, Sweet Meats business is thriving nicely. Maybe I should do both?"

"Both would be fine, whatever you want." Cotton rubbed up against her tummy, finally being rewarded with a scratch behind his ears. So far, so good, but she hadn't said what he wanted to hear yet. He knew she loved him. She let Darren go. She was figuring out her future.

But did it include him as more than just a nice pet?

"I think both then. No rush this time, I can work on weekends down on Bunny Hill, and weekdays at Sweet Meats." Candy nodded. "Yeah, I think that settles it." She moved away from the window and headed for the fridge. "What would you like for supper? I saw you chewing on that carrot grass when we were out delivering baskets."

Cotton's ears drooped further down again. "Oh, I don't know," his nose twitched. "I was thinking maybe some of the carrot grass with a side of-*am I just a pet or not?!*

Candy looked away from the refrigerator back at him. "If I am human and you are my cuddly bunny, you are my pet. When we are the same, we'll just see next time what happens."

That's all he needed to know as he took action. He watched as Candy danced around, trying to get out of her oversized clothes. "There, we are both bunny rabbits. So?"

Candy trotted away from her clothes, now back in her white fur with blonde streaks. She twitched her nose. Then started licking her paws and washing her face. Cotton wasn't going to just transform her into forgiveness. She watched him hop over towards her with a single untransformed basket. He laid it in front of her and transformed it.

"I made this for you, Candy."

Candy looked at the basket. It didn't have candy in it or a chocolate bunny. There were eggs, but they weren't real. "What are the fake eggs?"

"Something I tinkered with on the old conveyor belts." Cotton gestured to the two fake eggs. "You twist in the middle and they open. I wanted you to have it if you didn't throw me out."

Candy climbed into the basket and tried to hold the fake eggs with her paws. She held the bottom and the middle twisted easy. Inside were two tiny strange gold bands. "What are these?"

"We call them pinkerlings."

Pinkerlings? She picked one up and looked at it. What were they supposed to do?

"I really doubt I have an all out chance asking for anything else, but I wanted you to have one. It's the equivalent of . . .? Roses? Chocolates? Letter jackets?"

Candy moved herself to the second egg. She held the bottom with her body and twisted it with her front paws again. The whole top fell out of her hands and onto the carrot grass as she looked inside.

Another pinkerling? "Roses. Chocolates. Letter jackets." She looked at the funny egg pieces and noticed he placed BB and CS on them. "Silly Bunny, are you asking me to go steady with you?"

"Sort of? We could get married if-"

"Nope."

"Yeah, marriage isn't for us. Yet." He nosed the pinkerling. "One for each of us?"

They both wore one to show they were steady? Cute. "How do we put them on?"

It was the first time Candy had been cuddled up at her window with Cotton in her rabbit form. Watching the snow get lighter, they still wanted to cuddle up next to each other. Tucking her head below his, she thought for a moment over the last two crazy weeks she had. It was all worth it though. She wiggled her own cotton tail, still feeling the pinkerling around it. A magical band that never fell off until she took it off. As she moved her tiny tail, it also had this pinging noise that sounded like soft outdoor chimes clinking. "Do you think the snow will stop soon?"

"I am sure by tonight it will. True Spring has already started for us." Cotton nuzzled her gently with his nose. Nothing else was said between the two rabbits.

Year by year, Spring took over its rightful place. The word Easter Bunny was known on every child's lips as if there had always been such a thing. People picked up preparing for it as they did other holidays. They even colored their own eggs, just in case the rabbits didn't leave enough.

The supply of Easter Bunnies to keep the special day going each year only increased. Even Candy and Cotton added their own children to the mix when they eventually got married. They all tended to have Vegan magic.

Except for Butterscotch. Her daughter was vegan, but she didn't have the Vegan powers, she had the power of Sweet. No one understood how that could be, but Cotton and Candy didn't want to dwell on it.

Magic should have its own secrets, to keep wonder alive.

APOCALYPSE MOON CASTS JUDGMENT

Cheryl felt herself tumble across a room. She had never tumbled that far in her life. Groaning, she got her bearings and looked around. Guyver landed right beside her, moaning a bit himself. They were on a ground, frosted in some kind of crystal snow.

"I should kill you."

A voice. Cheryl turned and saw a teen girl who wore a green cloak that draped over her, sliding against the ground as she walked toward them. Her eyes spelled trouble though, glazed over and as frosted as the ground had been.

"I hate cold," she heard Guyver complain as he got up. He held his hand out to Cheryl and she took it.

"I should kill you. I should!" The girl stomped her foot and rubbed her nose. "What were you doing in there?"

"On Earth?" Cheryl questioned. "We were trying to find a new place to live. Our dimension was taken over."

"You hypocrite, how dare you speak to me with those words." Her voice was chilling. "You made me witness it. There's no going back now."

"Witness what?" Cheryl asked. Why was she so cross with her?

"This is not where you landed." The girl pointed behind them. Cheryl turned and saw a large dimension hole. "That is. You landed in my dimension right before it was lost."

"Oh. I am sorry," Cheryl answered. "I know how it feels. We've lost ours too."

"No, you ninny. I am the Apocalypse Moon! I have the chance to save dimensions, only if I don't see the ending." The girl sniffed. "There's nothing left in it. Even time doesn't tick. It's gone." She met Cheryl, eye to eye. "I can't save it and it's all your fault! What were you doing in there?"

"She already told you," Guyver said as he stood beside Cheryl. "We were trying to escape. Any harm we caused was on accident. Blaming us for this is pointless." Guyver would have spoke more, but Cheryl put her finger over his mouth, silencing him.

"Excuse me, but did you say your name was Apocalypse Moon?" Could she know Dominic? "Are you supposed to warn destined lovers?"

Apocalypse Moon took a step back. "There is no way one could know that information."

"My brother, Dominic," Cheryl said. "Before he stepped out of our dimension, a prophecy had called him the Apocalypse Sun. Have you met him?" Her eyes betrayed the truth. "You have? Is he okay?"

Apocalypse Moon looked conflicted as hair emerged in front of her eyes. She pushed it back along with her hood. "He is my enemy, yet he is a saver of my life. You are his sister, but you just destroyed my dimension." She stared at the ceiling. "What would my people want? Does it matter now that they no longer exist?"

She had seen him. "Is he okay?" Cheryl asked again. "He's quite shy. Not really used to making it out on his own."

"No, he's not." Apocalypse Moon stepped forward. "He is perfectly capable of his missions."

"I didn't mean it like that. He's . . .well, he's a good boy. He always had a thick shell around him though," she said hoping that conveyed her meaning.

"Then the shell broke. Apocalypse Sun is doing fine without you."

"Oh." He was already growing up. "He grew up quickly in a couple of days." Had it even been a couple of days? Had being removed from her propped him into a position where he was more self-confident?

"He is almost sixteen," Apocalypse Moon corrected her. "We move throughout time. You have been stuck in a dimension where time stopped moving."

"Sixteen?"

"Where are we?" Guyver interrupted. "Is this a safe dimension?"

"Everything is slowly dying, Apocalypse Sun and I are merely the threads trying to keep it together before everything unravels. Safe for now though, yes. However, not for long." Apocalypse Moon raised her hand toward them. "I am on the wish master path and I know now what is fair."

Cheryl felt wind coming from behind her. The dimension tunnel was changing to a purplish color. "What is that?"

"Apocalypse Sun saved me, yet he is my enemy. You are his sister, but you destroyed everything dear to me. This is only fair." The winds picked up from behind Apocalypse Moon. "I wish to send you two to the coldest dimension capable of sustaining life, where there is a good chance you will die if you don't find help. There you will live out the rest of your life in the bitter snow or you will brave it out and find the only dimension hole out of that miserable place and make it to a paradise. The fate is yours!"

"Wait!" Cheryl cried as she felt herself being blown backward. "What about my brother?"

"You will never see him again. I have placed this dimension hole with no return. Even I cannot rescue you later if I wanted too. Decide your own fate!" She yelled at them.

Cheryl almost got sucked in but fell into Guyver's back. He had found a pipe in the ground he was holding onto.

"This isn't what Apocalypse Sun would want," Guyver tried to reason. "He would want his family back. Cheryl is his only family!"

"You took out my whole dimension. My people!" She screamed back to them. "I work for the pride of my people. They raised me to be the Apocalypse Moon, to save dimensions, and there will never be a chance to save them. Unlike you two. I sense it." She looked toward both of them. "Salvation, that is what you are to each other. You survive because of each other. Then let it be fair." She held out her hand toward them. "Upon entering that dimension neither of you will know who you are or each other. You will have vague memories of your dimension, but nothing solid. I wish for you not to remember until you escape that dimension, if you do. "

"Not know each other?" Cheryl cried. Without knowing each other, why would they help each other? "Please, mercy! We are not responsible for what happened, it was an accident."

"Be happy I am being so kind as to letting your own strengths determine your fate." Apocalypse Moon held out her hand farther. "You can't cling forever."

Cheryl tried to hold onto the pipe, but it was too far. The winds were too heavy and Guyver was losing his grip.

"Go freeze in hell for what you've done to me."

"Then just send me. You don't need to take revenge against Cheryl," Guyver pleaded. "Dominic didn't even know me, there's no conflict of interest."

"No, don't say that." Cheryl looked toward him. "Guyver."

"Don't punish her. I take full responsibility."

"Kind words from an unkind act." Apocalypse Moon approached Cheryl. She grabbed her hand and yanked her away. "Try anything stupid and I will wish you to an early grave."

"Guyver?" Cheryl watched as he let go and tumbled into the other dimension. "Guyver!"

"Wait." Apocalypse Moon held her steady. Cheryl tried to fight the girl off, but she had incredible strength. "I am not some little girl you can mess around with and get away with it."

"What do you want?"

"It would be best to keep you here. Yet, I can't. Another dimension will suffer if I do."

"What do you mean? Aren't you wishing us dead?"

"I wish that I could get revenge without losing another dimension. I knew Guyver would give up like that for you though if he knew you'd go."

"Then you are just teasing us? Messing with us?"

"You deserve it. Now, go." Apocalypse Moon pushed her back as the winds came back. "I wasn't lying, but in order to make sure you survive he needed a headstart. Two years should be enough. You'll remember shortly after you see each other."

"Two years?"

"Yes and don't complain. If I were less passionate, I would have simply wished you dead." The last words echoed before the winds overcame her and she headed into another dimension.

THE SUN'S RAGE

Dominic lifted his head as he saw Apocalypse Moon. Her face was anything but happy to see him.

"Since you saved me from Nightmare King's grasp, I shall do you this favor." She looked above her. "I wish for Nightmare King not to interfere with me during my time here." She drew her attention back to Dominic. "Now you have no way to threaten me. You should not dare try because I am here only since you did save me. This is the honorable way so you should know. Crossing my enemy without him knowing it leads to lies and misdealings in the future."

Dominic approached her. "What have you done?"

"I met your sister and I sent her into a cold world in which she may never get out," she blurted toward him. "I placed a casting spell preventing you or I from reaching them."

Dominic stayed silent a moment. A sister. "I had a sister?"

"Apocalypse Moon! You do not tell him memories!"

"Her name was Cheryl," Apocalypse Moon stated, ignoring Nightmare King. "They fell into my dimension." She gestured toward herself. "My people's dimension! At the ending, right before it died. I have seen it and I cannot change it. You should feel lucky I did not kill her for such insolence."

"I have a sister." Dominic met her angry look with his own. He had family, and she . . ."I had a sister and you sent her away? You sent her away?!"

"See? I knew you would be upset."

"I can never see my family again, is that what you said about the dimension you just *brushed* her into?" Dominic shouted. "I have no memories, and now I *know* I have no family I can ever even meet. How could you? I even saved you from being here anymore, and this is how you repay me?"

"My dimension must die, forever and always, because of her. One life traded for countless billions." Apocalypse Moon lifted the hood on her cloak back over her head.

"And who else did you hurt?" Dominic questioned. "Did you hurt a 'him'? Someone that you will be endlessly sorry for? Because right now you should already feel endlessly sorry!"

"Her destined lover? I could not separate them."

"That's what you do after all. Hurt the destined lovers." Dominic drew his hands into fists. His own sister was a destined lover. One day, he could have found his way to her, before Apocalypse Moon. "Were you responsible for the chorus of leaves prophecy that got the first chosen killed?"

"I do what I have to do."

"You cold, selfish girl."

"You dare judge? What happened to that promise to step into my shoes!" she reminded him. "All the way back, when we were both there, you said that you would help me with a star-crossed love."

"I would have, if you didn't do this to me."

"Then that is that. That is your last favor from me." Apocalypse Moon began to fade. "We are always turned to enemies in the end. We cause nothing but hell for each other, so it was always written."

"We wouldn't be enemies if you didn't do that!" Dominic yelled at her as she faded away. "We'll see if that's the end of that." He held both his arms out and began to chant harsh tones.

"Stop!" Apocalypse Moon stopped fading and she ran right to him, but it was too late. "How did you even—?"

"Know how to summon him? You told me." Dominic's glare was cold. Even if he remembered his sister, he could never see her again. All because he had spared Apocalypse Moon.

"This stops now!" Nightmare King bellowed. Dominic watched as he manifested himself into a figure in a dark cloak. It was too late though. Dominic called for the Master of Wishes, taking Apocalypse Moon's way to travel.

"You are stranded again, but don't expect I will help you this time." Dominic crossed his arms. The scrolls showed him how to summon the master of wishes, but it warned his skill level could not handle it. He even tried, but failed. However, he could take the power for himself, an exchange. Whatever he wished, it could now be his. "I wish to return to Sera and warn her of the apocalypse!"

However, nothing happened. Apocalypse Moon no longer had the power, but the Master of Wishes did not listen.

"Deep in my lair, never. Never!" Nightmare King reached out to Dominic.

"I wish for Nightmare King to cause me no harm." Remembering Apocalypse Moon's words, Nightmare King stopped reaching for him.

"Stalemate, my enemy." Apocalypse Moon's eyes showed a moment of red before they went back to normal. "I cannot leave, but neither can you. We are once again prisoners."

There had to be a way to leave. Maybe not directly, but indirectly. "I wish to find a way to something that will let me reach the destination I want the most!"

FINDING THE REFLECTION PATH

The next moment, Dominic felt freedom. The freedom that he felt only in dreams. Looking around himself, he didn't quite understand where he was at. It was watery, but he stayed dry. The walls around him rippled like they were made of water. Remembering what Cupid said, he had an inkling of where he had been taken to. He had lost the master of wishes, but he was sent to something that could work.

"Who are you?"

Dominic turned as he heard a new voice. Light yet serious. He gestured to himself. "I am Apocalypse Sun."

"You are filth!" A strange nude woman wearing nothing but clothes of moving water approached him. "I am a water spirit, but I do not guide people like you."

Filth? Dominic wrinkled his nose. "I've been stuck with the Nightmare King for three and a half years, I wouldn't come out smelling like a cherry."

She took a step back. "That long?" She gasped and held her hand to her heart. "Your eyes are red and vicious. Your teeth are gnarled, and your hair is wild. You cannot be here on my path, someone with so much nightmare ability could not find the way."

Red? Dominic blinked. His eyes had turned red? He looked down at his clothes. Pure rags. At one time, they were beautiful. Mister

Umbrella gave him a wonderful outfit but it looked like it had been through hell and back. Tattered and worn, it barely covered his essentials anymore. In dreams, he always looked fresh and polished. In real life, he was surrounded in darkness and alone. His appearance was never on his mind.

He reached his hand to his head. His hair was oily and thick. He could have squeezed it and had fluid drop out. He regretted his words now. Biting his lip he looked at his arms. So crusted, so dark, and so dirty. "I . . ." He swallowed. "I must need a bath."

The watery woman came up to him closer. "Your eyes are changing color again." She brought her hand out to him, almost fearful, but laid her hand on his head. She shivered and pulled it away. "You kid not. You have lived years in the nightmare world."

How strange. When Dominic first met Nightmare King he didn't know what to do. He was never mean and always forgiving. As time went by he became bolder, and now he realized he'd been changing. "I'm not bad."

"I see." She removed her hand from his head. "You are not, but you must be cleansed, inside and out. Living inside Boogeyman's realm, it would affect anyone psychologically."

"So I am not who I even used to be?" Dominic gulped. "I never knew who I was, and now I don't even act like myself?"

"The deep anger will subside, but you will truly never become the person you were before the nightmare world." She clapped her fingers and swirled her hands. "Every day there you have grown worse. The last year the anger inside must have more than tripled. I will do my best to bring you your peace of mind back. I cannot give you your memories, he is more powerful than I." She swirled her hands to the left, then right, and then up.

Dominic watched as water rushed toward him from all sides. The force was so powerful it turned him around like he was stuck in a tornado. Water touched every piece of him as it rose him into the air.

It went up his nose, into his eyes, and through his ears. The water continued its vicious dance around him. He screamed as it invaded him deeper.

He could feel it swirling in his lungs and in his mouth. It came in and out of every orifice almost simultaneously, like water going through a straw. It pounded in his body ferociously.

Then, something changed. The water was still just as strong but there was no more pain. He felt his spirit reawakening. The water felt like the sun on a summer morning. Indescribably good. Before he had a chance to smile at the sensation, it departed from him.

The force no longer holding him up brought him to the ground. His hand reached out to the floor and his knees bent to keep him from collapsing.

Dominic looked down at his clothes. They sparkled like they were brand new. No longer dirty nor tattered, it was like Mister Umbrella in the Sky had just given them to him all over again.

Dominic raised his head. He felt the water from his hair slap the back of his neck as it poured down one more time, escaping down his back.

"Now, you are fit." The water woman smiled. "I mean, to take my pathway!" She touched her chest. "I didn't mean anything else, Apocalypse Man."

"It's boy," Dominic corrected her.

"Hon', when was the last time you looked in a mirror?" She snapped her fingers and the water trailing along the wall became still. Dominic turned and faced one.

That wasn't the face of a thirteen year old boy anymore. He was broad shouldered and surprisingly muscular for a sixteen year old. "How do I have that much muscle? I just worked in dreams."

"I imagine you worked in dreams hard." She came over to the back of him. "To even take a step takes great strength. You had to exert yourself every day. You could not see yourself covered in that darkness and filth, but that is you. That is the Apocalypse Man. Or teen? Certainly not boy though."

Dominic straightened his collar. "Traveler. Apocalypse Traveler, that's what people can call me from now on."

"Don't accept your chosen name? You were the one to choose it?" She shrugged. "Well, Apocalypse Traveler, it's time for you to be on your way." She pointed to one of the walls and the water rippled away, creating a hole. "Where is your destination?"

The only place he'd been wanting to get to since he was thirteen. The only thing he had left in his memories. The need to save someone in particular, that made him give everything up to Nightmare King. "Sera in the Lost and Found."

"Ooh." She pursed her lips together. "Even as strong as you are, I do not know if you can pierce Lost and Found. You may have to settle for mimicking until you get better."

"What is mimicking?"

"Your actions will be her actions. No matter what she does, you will mimic her. As you get better, you can eventually talk to her." She waved her hand towards him. "You may travel the path of reflection now. You will not always see her, but every time there is a reflection, contact will be made. Good luck, Apocalypse Traveler."

"What about after her?" Dominic had to ask. He did not want to ever go back to Nightmare King again.

"Your path is fate. It will find you."

That explanation was no explanation, but it would have to do. Heading out past the watery walls, he headed into a strange green pasture. As he walked, he realized he couldn't stop.

He was on the reflection path now and he'd have no control of himself until he got stronger.

The Sun's rage at the Moon, prophecy foretold? Honestly, a little lame of a prophecy. Hindering Sun's sister certainly created a rift between them, but it's not like she even killed her. Plus, Moon was dealing with some issues of her whole meaning of existence now gone.

A prophecy is not something small like a cute friendship falling apart, it is foretold of great things. There have been many Apocalypse Messengers in time, and most never even met, let alone got along. Why would a spat between Sun and Moon be so greatly important?

I don't trust this, do you?

You know, at least the bunnies got their little pinkerlings and happy ending and didn't die in the rough snow.

You have no idea how rough that snow can get when the darkness creeps in.

Did you finish your tale? Want more now in the Sun and Moon Adventure series?

You can collect individual books or you can also buy bundles to collect easier if you prefer.

Who is Sun and Moon? Sun and Moon may or may not feature in each book. Younger adventures especially don't feature them as much. Sun and Moon start as children and grow up into adults through your many adventures. This series will have them just from the ages of 12-16. There are more series featuring them in the future.

The best way to enjoy the books is simply to join my patreon. For a small fee per month, you can read all of the books that are currently there. I mean with the ebook copies that I actually sell, you will be able to download those to your own devices. Other books will have posted chapter by chapter.

Want to follow the journey but really don't want to pick up the next book? (Not a big fan of what the next book will be.) There will be a story thus far page at https://www.patreon.com/posts/153020946 that is open to free members and non-members alike. You can select the book you wanted to skip, and get the full spoilers of the book there, so you can stay caught up.

Each book also has a print cover, including the bundles. Die hard fans can in fact read these adventures in print.

I love giving away free books to bring more readers into my world. Keep your eyes peeled on my patreon page for any giveaways, especially around the holidays.

Thank you for joining my worlds! I hope you have a great emotional journey that stays with you for years to come.

-Serena Walken

Don't miss out!

Visit the website below and you can sign up to receive emails whenever Serena Walken publishes a new book. There's no charge and no obligation.

https://books2read.com/r/B-A-TPG-LJJXB

BOOKS2READ

Connecting independent readers to independent writers.

Did you love *For Love of Mister Cotton Tail: A Closed Door Romantasy Easter Novella*? Then you should read *Finding Home: A Closed Door Romantasy Novella*[1] by Serena Walken!

[2]

When you didn't feel for your destined the day your dimension ended, can you still be with them without feeling regret?

Cheryl's life gets flipped around when her whole town disappeared without her or her brother. She gets a visit from someone who claims they can help them, and heads into a new life only to find herself not gaining anything, but losing everything. Losing in every way possible. With the bittersweet knowledge she holds now though, can she really find a new place to call her home and move on with her life, when everything she once cared for is gone?

---

1. https://books2read.com/u/b5eMKR

2. https://books2read.com/u/b5eMKR

Word count: 27k. A collection of Cheryl and Guyver's relationship through the books have been assembled for a full HEA. Also includes the ending to their own journey.

Read more at https://serenawalken.net.

Also by Serena Walken

A Sun and Moon Adventure
When the Faeries Start to Fall: A Closed Door Romantasy Novella
Project Wolf: A Closed Door Romantasy Shifter Novella
Saving Mrs. Claus: A Closed Door Romantasy Christmas Novella
Game World: A Closed Door Romantasy Novella
In A Chorus of Falling Leaves: A Closed Door Romantasy Novella
Missing Cupid: A Closed Door Romantasy Valentine Novella
Wonderland Mafia: A Closed Door Romantasy Novella
For Love of Mister Cotton Tail: A Closed Door Romantasy Easter
Novella
Finding Home: A Closed Door Romantasy Novella
Branded: A Closed Door Romantasy Novella

From The World Of Dead Faerie Tales
Fear and Firecrackers

Lost Secret Series
Death by Cake
Death by Cupcake
Death by Sweet Tarts

Watch for more at https://serenawalken.net.

About the Author

Serena Walken loves to write fantasy, sometimes whimsical or sometimes dark. She lives in Kansas with her wonderful daughter but will (hopefully) in a few years be living in Canada.

https://serenawalken.net and https://www.patreon.com/cw/authorserenawalken is where you can find more books and writing of hers. Patreon and smashwords can get you her ebooks cheaper or even sometimes free.

Serena Walken's work can be found at Webnovel and other online places (sometimes read free, sometimes for coins.) She tries to provide print copies to her books big and small as well.

Read more at https://serenawalken.net.